all
fall
dow<small>n</small>

BUSSELTON SENIOR HIGH SCHOOL

LIBRARY

Susan Geason was born in Tasmania, grew up in Queensland, and now lives in Sydney. Most of her professional life has centred on politics and writing, including positions as a researcher in Parliament House, Canberra and Cabinet Adviser in the NSW Premier's Department. Since 1988 she has worked as a freelance writer and editor, including a five-year stint from 1992–1997 as literary editor of Sydney's *Sun-Herald*. Her crime fiction for adults has been published around the world in several languages. Her first book for teenagers, *Great Australian Girls* (1999), was very successful, and was followed by a companion volume, *Australian Heroines* (2001).

She recently completed a PhD in Creative Writing at the University of Queensland.

Susan can be contacted by email: susan@susangeason.com

all
fall
down

R HIGH SCHOOL

F
GEA

LIBRARY

Susan Geason

LITTLE HARE

Acknowledgment
Thanks to Ali Lavau for the adverbs, the history of cement, bicycle lore, and the pep talks.

Little Hare Books
4/21 Mary Street, Surry Hills
NSW 2010 AUSTRALIA

www.littleharebooks.com

Copyright © Susan Geason 2005

First published in 2005

All rights reserved. No part of this publication may be reproduced, stored in a retrieval system or transmitted in any form or by any means, electronic, mechanical, photocopying, recording or otherwise, without the prior written permission of the publisher.

National Library of Australia
Cataloguing-in-Publication entry

Geason, Susan, 1946– .
All fall down.

ISBN 1 877003 86 7.

1. Teenage girls – Juvenile fiction. 2. Kidnapping victims
– Juvenile fiction. 3. Sydney (N.S.W.) – Social conditions
– Juvenile fiction. I. Title.

A823.3

Cover design by Louise McGeachie
Set in 13.5/17.5pt Adobe Garamond by Asset Typesetting Pty Ltd
Printed and bound in Australia by Griffin Press, Adelaide

Cover image of girl reproduced by kind permission
of the Roger Vaughan Picture Library.

Cover image of Windmill Street showing the Hero of Waterloo
reproduced by kind permission of State Records of NSW: CGS 4481,
Glass Negatives, [Aperture Card 1096]

Map of the City of Sydney (page vi) held in
the Mitchell Library, State Library of New South Wales

5 4 3 2 1

This one is for Rose and Hazel Peterson

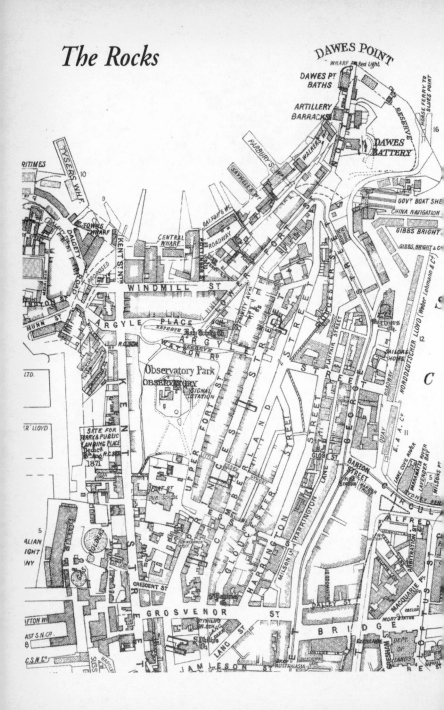

The Rocks

DAWES POINT

WHARF — Red Light

Dawes Pt
BATHS

ARTILLERY
BARRACKS

DAWES
BATTERY

HORSE FERRY TO
BLUES POINT

RESERVE

16

GOVᵀ BOAT SHE

CHINA NAVIGATION

GIBBS BRIGHT

GIBBS, BRIGHT & Cᵒ

NORDDEUTSCHER LLOYD (Weber Lohmann & Cᵒ)

C

RITIMES

TYSERS WHᶠ

10

9

FOWES
WHARF

DALGETY

KENT STᴺ

CENTRAL
WHARF

BALTOWS Wᴴ

ROADWAY

PARBURY'S

WALKER'S WF

PROPOSED

WINDMILL ST

MUNN ST

ARGYLE PLACE

R.C. CH

ARGY

WATSON Rᵈ

RESERVE

12

SAILORS
HOME

LTD.

Observatory Park
OBSERVATORY
SIGNAL
STATION

er LLOYD

SITE FOR
FERRY & PUBLIC
LANDING PLACE
Dedice
24 Aug. R.C. SER
1871

PORT ST
PUB. SCHOOL

QUAY

E. & A. Cᵒ

11

LANE COVE RIVER

PARRAMATTA RIVER

LAVENDER BAY

MILSONS POINT

5

ALIAN
IGHT
NY

CRESCENT ST

GROSVENOR ST

GLOUCESTER LANE

HARRINGTON

MILSON

BARTON
STREET

GLOBE ST

ALFRED

MACQUARIE PL

OBELISK

MORT STATUE

BRIDGE
OF
LANDS

DEPT.
OF
LANDS

AFTON Wᴴ

AST S.N.Cᵒ

C.S.N.Cᵒ

SUSS

NAPOLI

Sᵀ PHILIP
PR. SCH

Sᵀ PHILIPS
CH.

LANG ST

GROSVENOR ST

JAMIESON ST

AUSTRALASIA

GRESHAM ST

FIRE
STATION

SYDNEY HARBOR

...R HIGH SCHOOL
LIBRARY

chapter one

The tantalising aroma of baking cakes lured Christabel McManus downstairs. With the huge wood-fuelled stove blasting out more heat than the engines of hell, the kitchen was like an inferno.

As if January in Sydney isn't hot enough already, Christabel thought irritably. Plonking herself down at the pine table, she watched Mrs Cadwallader beating eggs, sugar and flour in an enormous white bowl clutched to her capacious bosom, the occasional bead of sweat dropping off the end of her nose. Christabel wondered if it would make the sponge taste salty.

"I'm bored, Caddie," she moaned, sliding off her shoes to cool her stockinged feet on the floor tiles.

"You're always bored," said the cook. "Go and read one of your school books, or do your fancy work."

Christabel groaned. She hated sewing with a passion, and had calculated that, at her current rate of progress, the grubby tablecloth she was pretending to embroider would be finished when she turned sixty-seven. "It's too hot. I'll just leave dirty finger marks all over it. And I'm certainly not going to do any study in the school holidays!"

The cook had heard all this before. She sighed. "Do you want to scrape the bowl?"

"Oh, Caddie, I'm far too old for that!"

"Then help me with the baking, Miss Hoity Toity," said Mrs Cadwallader; the prospect of work could usually dislodge Christabel from the kitchen.

Just then Katie Cadwallader came in through the back door, looking half dead. From George Street, in the city centre, she had walked through the park known as the Domain, down past the art gallery to the wharves of Woolloomooloo and up the stairs to Wylde Street in Potts Point, where Altona, the McManus family home, stood. Her mother hastened to pour her a glass of lemonade.

"Katie!" said Christabel, pleased to see a new face. She had known Katie, a tall well-built girl with fair hair and a round, pretty, shiny-apple face, all her young life. Something was different about the cook's daughter today, though . . . Then Christabel saw what it was: despite the heat, Katie was wearing an unflattering, long-sleeved, dark blue suit buttoned to the neck and a dowdy bonnet. "What *is* that strange outfit you've got on?!"

Flushing with embarrassment, Katie said, "I've joined the Salvation Army, Miss Christabel."

"The what?"

"It's a new church—" Katie began, only to be interrupted by Mrs Lovelock, the housekeeper, who swept into the kitchen and announced that Maggie Rafferty, one of the maids, had disappeared.

"Do you know anything about this, Cook?" she demanded. A tall, thin, ramrod-straight woman in her fifties with black hair scraped into a bun, the house-keeper somehow managed to make the maid's disappearance seem like Mrs Cadwallader's fault.

Out of the corner of her eye, Christabel saw Katie Cadwallader stiffen, but the cook simply turned, wiped her hands on her apron, and said calmly, "No, Mrs Lovelock, just what you've told us now."

"This is too bad," huffed the housekeeper, jingling her huge ring of keys angrily. "Leaving without a word. What could have happened to make Maggie behave so thoughtlessly?"

"Perhaps a family emergency," suggested Katie meekly.

Mrs Lovelock pursed her thin lips. "Well, I can't stand around all day gossiping. I shall have to contact an agency and see if we can get a replacement. Until then, we shall all have to pitch in."

When she'd gone, the tension in the room evaporated.

"You know something, don't you, Katie?" Christabel said accusingly. "I saw that look on your face. What's happened?"

"It's Paddy, Maggie's little boy . . ."

"Is he ill?"

"No, he's gone."

Christabel had met Paddy from time to time when his grandmother brought him to the house to visit his mother. She had been charmed by his cheeky face and dark curls. "Gone! What do you mean, gone?"

Katie gave her mother a beseeching look. "You'll have to tell her," said Mrs Cadwallader. "Once she gets the bit between the teeth there's no stopping her. She'll nag me ragged if you don't."

"His father took him."

"But his father's dead!"

"No, I'm afraid Sean Rafferty is alive and kicking," said Katie.

"But I thought Maggie was a widow."

"She said that to get the job, Miss," explained Katie. "Mrs Lovelock wouldn't have hired her if she'd known she had a husband out there somewhere. Especially not a husband like Sean Rafferty."

"Why, what's he like?" asked Christabel curiously.

"Good-looking, popular with the ladies . . . You'd think butter wouldn't melt in his mouth," said the cook scornfully. "But he's always thought himself too high and mighty to work for a living like everyone else. Maggie put up with his drinking and gambling, but when Sean started running with a gang of thieves and brawlers just after she'd had Paddy, she left him."

Christabel was shocked. She had never heard of a woman leaving her husband. Though now she thought about it, some of her father's married friends did spend long periods apart . . .

"She went back to her family, the O'Riordans," Mrs Cadwallader went on. "There's some would have sent her back to her husband, but they're good people and took her in. They're poor as church mice, though, so she had to go out to work to support herself and pay the boy's way. Her mother has been looking after him."

In the three years that Maggie had been working for the McManus family and living in the servants' quarters, Christabel had never given a thought to the maid's life outside the house or to her family. She'd never wondered what had happened to Maggie's husband, or if she missed her little boy. For the first time it occurred to her that Maggie must have been very unhappy. "Have they called in the police?" she asked.

Katie Cadwallader shook her head. "There's no point, Miss Christabel. They won't step in between a man and his wife, and they'll say the boy's father has as much right to him as his mother."

"But if he's a thief?!"

"Maggie is still married to him, and he's head of the family. If she fights him, he'll win."

"That can't be right!" Christabel was outraged.

"Maybe not, but I'm afraid that's the way it is."

Christabel had to admit the truth of what Katie said. Men seemed to rule the roost in most families she knew. "What about Maggie's family? Can't they do anything?" she asked.

"I'm sure they'll try," said Mrs Cadwallader. "The O'Riordans are a rough lot—they work on the wharves—but they're no match for Sean Rafferty."

"What Mum means is that they're nowhere near cunning enough to outwit Sean," explained Katie.

"But what would a man like that want with a little boy, Katie?" Christabel asked, bewildered.

"Paddy's about eight now, so he's old enough to be put to work. Sean will probably teach him to pick pockets. He's a dab hand at dipping himself."

"But that's terrible. He's such a sweet little boy!"

"He won't stay that way for long," predicted Mrs Cadwallader grimly. "His father won't look after him, so he'll have to shift for himself. He'll toughen up pretty quick."

"If Paddy gets caught, he'll end up in a reformatory," added Katie. "And if he isn't a thorough villain going in, he'll be one when he comes out." She got up to leave.

"But you didn't tell me about this army!" protested Christabel, watching Katie tie on her awful bonnet.

"I'm sorry, Miss, but I have work to do. We've got a soup kitchen on tonight, and after that a prayer meeting." Her eyes sparkled. "And band practice."

Christabel's eyebrows flew up. All the churches she'd been in had boring old organs and choirs. "You have a band?"

Katie nodded proudly. "A brass band. I only play the tambourine and sing so far, but I'm going to learn the trombone."

Watching her go, Christabel simmered with resentment. Why should a cook's daughter be allowed to run around Sydney by herself and play in a band when she couldn't leave the house without a chaperone? *Imagine what Papa would say if I learned to play the trombone,* she thought. *That's if he even noticed.*

She flounced into the parlour and took out her frustration on the Steinway, banging away at the keys till Sissy, the family cocker spaniel, leapt up and fled whining to the garden. Then her governess, Harriet Swift, appeared at the door and suggested that if she didn't have anything more useful to do, Christabel could always spend an hour on French conjugation, holidays or no holidays.

Since anything was preferable to French verbs, Christabel retreated to the garden, where she sat on the swing and thought about what had happened to little Paddy. It seemed terribly unjust that the boy's father could just up and take him and get away with it. Someone should go and take him back, Christabel decided. Someone smarter than the O'Riordans. Someone like Christabel McManus . . .

That afternoon, Christabel's friend Laura Primrose stopped by. She had spent the morning at the town hall, where she and her mother were helping to organise an exhibition of women's arts and crafts. Unlike most of Sydney's well-off families, the Primroses didn't go to the Blue Mountains or the Southern Highlands during the summer holidays. Mr Primrose was too busy with his law practice, and Mrs Primrose was equally busy with her hospital visiting, the evening school for factory girls she'd established and, of course, the Womanhood Suffrage League, which was campaigning to secure the vote for women.

There was never the slightest chance that the McManus family would leave the city. The hot weather seemed to breed diseases, and as Christabel's father, Dr Roderick McManus, was the Government Inspector of Health for New South Wales, he was kept busy fighting outbreaks of cholera, typhoid and gastroenteritis. Sometimes Christabel thought that if only she'd come down with some horrid disease, she might manage to catch his attention. Since the death of Christabel's mother two years earlier—from an infection she'd brought home from a community centre in Surry Hills, where she did charity work with Mrs Primrose—he was hardly ever at home. And even when he *was* home he was completely preoccupied with work. It made Christabel feel lonely and abandoned, and sometimes a little angry, too. He might have lost his wife, but she'd lost her mother!

As Hetty Primrose was raising her daughter to be independent, Laura arrived alone on foot, as usual. She bounced onto the verandah looking hot and dishevelled, tossed her hat onto a chair, and declared she was parched. Though they'd been best friends forever, as their mothers had been before Estella McManus's death, Laura and Christabel were opposites in looks and character. Christabel was impulsive and passionate, whereas Laura was serious and cautious; Laura was tall, dark and gangling, where Christabel was petite and blonde; Christabel was fascinated by clothes and fashion, while Laura would wear anything as long as it was clean and neat.

The girls threw themselves into cane chairs in the shade and Christabel rang a little brass bell for refreshments. Ten minutes later a maid brought out lemonade, sandwiches and slices of Mrs Cadwallader's famous jam roll.

"Who's that?" asked Laura. "Is she new?"

"I don't know," said Christabel, pouring her friend a glass of lemonade. "She must be a temporary.

Mrs Lovelock was looking for a replacement because Maggie Rafferty's gone."

"Why?" asked Laura through a mouthful of egg and watercress sandwich. "Couldn't she put up with you for another minute?"

Christabel was used to being teased by Laura, and didn't rise to the bait. "It turns out Maggie's not a widow after all, but has a husband who's a thief and a gambler. He's kidnapped their little boy from his grandmother's house to turn him into a pickpocket, and Maggie's gone to try to find him."

"That's awful! The poor woman. I suppose the family is scouring Sydney looking for him. Mind you, I don't see what they can do if it's his father who has taken him."

"Take him back, of course," said Christabel.

"But what good would that do? You can't play pass the parcel with a child."

Christabel wasn't listening. "I think we should try to get him back."

Laura stopped chewing and her brown eyes widened. "We? Who?"

"Me."

"Why?"

"It's wrong."

The determined look on Christabel's face alarmed Laura. "All sorts of things are wrong, Belle," she said. "You can't run around trying to fix everything."

"Why not, Lolly? Your mother does it all the time."

"But she's a grown-up! You're fourteen! Anyway, why are you so worked up about it?"

"Paddy's a dear little boy. He's almost part of the family."

Laura eyed her suspiciously. "I don't believe you. Besides Miss Swift, the only servant here who's part of the family is Caddie, and that's only because she's irreplaceable. My mother always says a good cook is worth her weight in rubies."

Christabel was offended. "But I love Caddie!"

"Because she spoils you rotten and mothers you. You treat the rest of them like furniture. You knew nothing about Maggie whatever-her-name-is, and cared less, until it suited you."

"That's unfair, Lol!" But, secretly, Christabel wondered if her friend might be right.

Taking pity, Laura gave her friend a hug. "I'm sorry, Belle. I didn't mean to hurt your feelings." Then she jumped up and put on her hat. "I have to go or I'll miss my tram from town."

Christabel walked her to the gate and, after they'd kissed goodbye, Laura said, "You're not going to hare off after Paddy Rafferty, are you? It's really none of your business and, if Sean Rafferty is as bad as you say, he could be dangerous."

Christabel's face took on a stubborn look.

Laura groaned. "Promise me you won't do anything silly, Belle. I don't want to open the paper and read that you've been beaten up by larrikins and left bleeding in an alleyway."

"No, Lol. I can't promise you anything," Christabel said obstinately, and turned and walked back up the driveway.

chapter two

Although Christabel occasionally thought about Paddy Rafferty's plight, she did nothing about it for the next couple of days. She was kept fully occupied planning her wardrobe for an outing to the Palace Theatre to see a new production of *A Midsummer Night's Dream*, which had received rave reviews and was drawing huge crowds.

Dr McManus had promised to take the girls himself as a birthday present for Laura but, when the day came, he was called away to an emergency meeting with the Minister for Health. Not for the first time, Christabel's governess, Harriet Swift, had to chaperone the girls in his place.

Christabel loved the theatre—the crystal chandeliers, gilded cherubs and giant pots of flowers; the hum of anticipation; the heady aroma of women's scents and powders and men's pomades; the cavalcade of the latest hairdos and fashions; and the sense of entering another world when the lights went down. She particularly liked the Palace, which looked as if it had been built for an Indian rajah. Because it was a special occasion, tonight she and Laura would be perched above the audience in one of the side boxes that looked like miniature Hindu temples. It was Christabel's first time in a theatre box, and the velvet curtains, blue and gold satin furnishings, and gilded spire combined to make her feel like an Indian princess, especially when she looked down on the dress circle below. When the play started, Christabel gave herself up completely to the illusion and was soon far away.

At intermission, with Christabel deploying her sharp elbows and Miss Swift in their wake, the girls battled their way through the crush to the foyer for refreshments, then moved to the side of the room to watch the passing parade. All of Sydney seemed to be out tonight. Since the end of the economic recession two years before, people had money to spend again, as was evident from the finery on display at the theatre. Not that it was all in the best of taste, as Christabel was quick to point out. She herself was dressed in apple-green satin and a peridot necklace, which brought out the green in her eyes, and even

Laura had made an effort in blue shot silk with a cyclamen sash and her mother's amethysts. Despite Harriet Swift's admonitions, Christabel kept up a running commentary on the women's clothes and hair till the bell rang, making Laura laugh so hard she spilled her creaming soda.

After the play, they emerged into the street, surprised to find themselves in Sydney in 1900 rather than a fairy kingdom, and began dissecting the costumes, the sets and the performances.

"I wish I could turn people into asses with a magic spell like Puck did," said Christabel.

"Why? Most people seem perfectly capable of turning themselves into asses," remarked Laura.

"Girls, don't be so rude," said Miss Swift.

The girls were still giggling when a flurry of movement nearby caught Christabel's attention. She turned just in time to see a small boy deliberately bump into a large, slightly inebriated man who had stopped to light a cigar. The man gave a grunt and swore at the boy, who ran off without an apology. The boy was Paddy Rafferty!

With a cry of recognition, Christabel hiked up her skirts and took off after him, ignoring her governess's objections. Under normal circumstances, she was sure she could have caught him but, hampered by tight shoes and petticoats, Christabel was too slow. Paddy quickly outpaced her and turned into a laneway.

When Christabel reached the mouth of the alley, she hesitated. It was dark and forbidding. Anybody could be waiting for her in there. Deciding that discretion was the better part of valour, she gave up.

By this time Miss Swift and Laura had caught up with her. "Look at you!" the governess scolded. "I just hope none of your father's friends saw you."

Christabel wasn't listening. "Katie was right," she said, still breathing hard. "Paddy's father is teaching him to pick pockets."

After she had calmed down and fixed her hair, the threesome walked back to the theatre, where they found the groom, Tom Cartwright, guarding their carriage. As it was a warm windless night, Tom put the carriage top down. With Sultan, the glossy black stallion, in the traces, Christabel and Laura felt like visiting royalty—until a group of larrikins in Oxford Street called them Lady Mucky-Mucks. The girls were appalled at first, then Christabel gave them the haughty wave favoured by the Governor's wife.

"Christabel, please behave yourself," warned Miss Swift, but the girls were laughing too hard to hear.

When Cartwright dropped Laura off at her house in Woollahra, Christabel said in a lock-jawed English accent, "Good night, Lady Muck," and the girls broke down again.

On the way home Miss Swift delivered a lecture on ladylike behaviour that lasted most of the journey. Christabel, to whom it was as familiar as the multiplication table, shut it out and turned her mind to rescuing Paddy. Suddenly her dreams of rescuing him were no longer just an idle distraction. She had to do something—but what? She was never allowed out alone. It would be different if she were a boy . . . The regular clip-clop of Sultan's hooves brought her back to the present—and gave her an idea.

"You're not going to tell on me, are you, Swiftie?" she cajoled as they rolled into the driveway of Altona.

"Not this time," said Miss Swift.

Christabel sighed with relief.

A well-brought-up clergyman's daughter from Kent in England, Harriet Swift was an intelligent young woman with a good sense of humour. Although Swiftie was officially Christabel's governess, she also acted as a companion and older sister figure to the motherless girl, and had almost become part of the family. Christabel tried her best not to goad Swiftie beyond endurance but did not always succeed. When they were getting along well, she was grateful for Harriet's presence; when they disagreed, she prayed the governess's fiancé would return from that plantation in Fiji and marry her. Then perhaps her father would allow her to go to Sydney Girls High School with Laura. She'd been nagging for a year now, but to no avail. Her father refused to consider the idea, saying that her mother and his sisters in Edinburgh had been educated at home and, if it was good enough for them, it was good enough for his daughter.

Next morning, Christabel slipped out to the stables on the pretext of taking some carrots to Stepper, the McManus's amiable chestnut gelding. She brushed him down, plaited some braids into his mane and fed him, all the time keeping an eagle eye on the groom's movements. Grateful for all the attention, Stepper butted her gently with his big head, and tried to nibble her ear.

When Tom Cartwright went up to the house for a cup of tea at eleven, Christabel gave the horse one last pat then went looking for Billy Brownlow. She found the stable boy in Sultan's stall. Christabel, who gave the temperamental Sultan a wide berth, had to admire Billy's way with the stallion. Thirteen-year-old Billy was small and wiry, with flaming red hair, guileless blue eyes and freckles. Seeing Christabel, he blushed furiously.

"Billy," said Christabel sweetly.

"Yes, Miss?"

"Do you remember how you lent me some of your clothes for the play at Christmas?"

"Ye-e-s," the boy said cautiously.

"Well, I want to borrow them again."

"What for, Miss?"

"That's my affair," said Christabel dismissively.

Billy's eyes narrowed. "Then I'm afraid I can't help you."

"Why not?!"

"I know you, Miss. You'll get up to no good, and if ya get caught, I'll get in trouble for helping you."

"No one'll find out, Billy."

"That's what you say, but the doctor's got eyes in the back of 'is 'ead. When you run away to Miss Primrose's last year because he wouldn't let ya go to school, he had ya back 'ere before ya could say Jack Robinson."

Christabel felt like stamping her foot in irritation, but she recalled Caddie's maxim about catching more flies with honey than vinegar. Christabel asked herself what Billy's honey might be, and the answer came to her immediately. "I'll pay you a pound," she said.

Billy's eyes popped—he'd never had a pound in his pocket in his life. "Where would you get a quid from, Miss?"

"After I ran away, Papa raised my allowance to keep me quiet, and I've been saving it up for emergencies. This is one."

"What is, Miss?"

"None of your business. The less you know the better. That way, if anybody asks questions, you won't have to tell any lies. You're a terrible liar."

Billy reddened again. It was true; his face was an open book. But he was also stubborn. "No trade then," he said, and went on with mucking out Sultan's stall.

Christabel longed to slap him, but knew this would ruin her plans. There was no choice but to tell the truth. "All right, Billy. I'm going to look for Paddy Rafferty in The Rocks, but if I go there as myself nobody will tell me anything."

21

Billy's eyes widened. "So ya wanta go in as a boy?"

Christabel nodded.

Billy looked her up and down, noting the straight lines, and said, "I suppose you'd pass."

It was Christabel's turn to blush now. She knew she hadn't started developing yet, but she didn't need stable boys pointing out her lack of feminine allure. She needed Billy's help, though, so instead of getting on her high horse, she said, "It's a deal, then."

"One pound, and I come too," said Billy, pressing his advantage.

"No!" said Christabel. The cheek!

"Then it's no go, Miss. I'm not lettin' ya go into The Rocks by yerself."

From the determined look on Billy's face it was clear that he was not going to give in, so Christabel had to. "All right," she conceded, vowing to herself that she would get rid of him later.

"It's me 'alf-day off termorrer, and I'm goin' 'ome to see Mum," Billy said. "I'll bring ya back some of me old clothes."

"And a big cap," said Christabel.

Just then Tom Cartwright turned up and, seeing Billy leaning on his pitchfork, shouted at him to leave Miss McManus alone, stop yapping and get back to work!

Christabel gave Billy a hard look to warn him not to renege, and went back into the house to practise talking in a gruff voice and walking like a boy in front of a mirror.

chapter three

The house was finally quiet. The servants, who had to rise at dawn, were all in bed by nine. At ten, Miss Swift had put away her embroidery and told Christabel, who'd been pretending to read, to go up to bed.

Twanging with impatience and tension, Christabel paced her large airy bedroom like a caged tiger. She stuck some autographs and theatre programs into her scrapbook, then threw herself onto the lacy cushions scattered across her four-poster bed and tried to read a magazine. In the end she gave up trying to distract herself, and sat on the window seat overlooking the driveway watching for her father's return.

Eventually, she heard the sound of his carriage, then his footsteps on the gravel drive and the front door opening, and finally his tread on the stairs as he came up to bed. She gave him half an hour to settle, then began her preparations.

First she donned Billy's cast-off shirt, knicker-bockers, socks and boots. The boots, which were rather pongy, were also a couple of sizes too big, so she stuffed the toes with pages torn from her magazine—she wouldn't be able to run with blisters. Into one of the boots she slipped a pound note folded very small. After braiding her hair tightly and pinning it close to her head, she put on Billy's second-best cap, pulled it down to shade her eyes, and snarled menacingly at herself in the mirror. Then she snapped the braces that held up her trousers and grinned. Apart from the fact that she was a little too clean, she looked like any other street urchin in Sydney. Finally, she put a handkerchief pilfered from her father's chest of drawers into her pocket.

When her father's deafening snores began to rip through the house, Christabel took a deep breath and climbed out of the window onto the roof. The ground was a long way down. She began to inch her way carefully down the giant Moreton Bay fig to the garden below.

The moment she let go of the lowest branch and dropped to the ground, a shape materialised out of the gloom, startling her. She would have screamed if she hadn't recognised Billy, signalling to her to be quiet. Silently, they set off for the street. When they were out of earshot of the house, Billy said, "You could've fooled me, Miss. You look just like me little brother, Ernie."

All business, Christabel ignored what she supposed was meant to be a compliment. "Which way should we go, Billy?" she demanded.

"It's faster through the Domain, but I'm not goin' in there at night. It's too dangerous."

"Dangerous?! How?"

"Them coves from the Woolloomooloo Push don't like strangers on their turf. They'd bash us up just fer the fun of it. We'll have to go the long way round."

Christabel shivered. She had heard about the pushes, the gangs of larrikins that were terrorising the working-class neighbourhoods and making many of Sydney's back alleys unsafe. They also staged legendary battles armed with broken bottles, knives and fists. Maybe this wasn't such a good idea . . . But Billy was striding on, so she hurried to catch up with him. This was her idea, and she'd have to see it through. Besides, she would rather die than look like a coward.

As they trudged down the narrow streets of Darlinghurst, most of them dark and empty except for a few drunks staggering home, Christabel outlined her plan. "I think you should go into some pubs and ask after Sean Rafferty, Billy. Someone will know where he lives."

"Nah, that won't work. Them folks don't know me, so they won't tell me nuthin'. We'll go and see me auntie. She knows everybody in The Rocks. And their business."

"Where does your auntie live?"

"She's got a shop in Windmill Street."

As they passed St Mary's Cathedral, Christabel recalled what she'd read in the newspaper about The Rocks. On the one hand, there were the respectable residents, like his aunt, who worked in the boarding houses, shops and pubs as seamstresses, laundresses, bootmakers, butchers and bakers, or as labourers on the wharves at Circular Quay and Walsh Bay. But because it abutted the port, The Rocks swarmed with sailors desperate for a good time after months at sea, and the locals were only too happy to relieve them of their hard-earned pay. Every vice was on sale at The Rocks, which was awash with drugs and alcohol, and thronging with thieves, prostitutes and touts of all kinds. The place sounded like another country, a law unto itself, with its own harsh codes of behaviour.

These tales of evil and danger sounded exciting to Christabel, though her excitement was tinged with fear. She just hoped that her disguise would hold up! She was starting to feel grateful that she had Billy to guide her.

They made their way past exclusive Macquarie Street with its mansions overlooking the Botanic Gardens, and into George Street. From there they skirted the wharves of Circular Quay and trekked past shops and rows of warehouses till they reached the Argyle Cut, where they turned left into The Rocks.

As they plunged deeper into The Rocks, the stink hit Christabel like a sledgehammer, and she almost gagged on the noxious stew of blocked drains and tannery waste, all overlaid with the insidious reek of raw sewage. Her first reaction was to pull her father's handkerchief from her pocket and hold it to her nose, but Billy dashed her hand away.

"Don't do that, Miss," he whispered urgently. "You'll look like ya don't belong."

Chastened, Christabel shoved the hanky back into her pocket, and tried to take in her surroundings without staring too rudely. The narrow streets and lanes were crammed with shops and tenement buildings with tiny windows. Between them were mean, whitewashed, one-storey row cottages, two-storey terraces with one room up and one down, and pubs and workshops. Many of the front doors were open—so the inhabitants could breathe, Christabel guessed; in this heat the cramped hovels would be stifling. And the noise was deafening. The sound of singing and shouting spilled from the doorways of the public houses, dogs barked, carriages rolled over the cobbles, and women screamed at children to "Git 'ome!" The tranquillity and order of Potts Point seemed a continent away.

The streets were thronging with people—Lascars with mahogany faces and earrings; weather-beaten Englishmen with cockney accents; tall Americans, probably off a whaling ship; sailors of various types; argumentative larrikins in sharp suits; gaudily dressed women with painted faces and tired eyes; exhausted labourers on their way home; and, despite the late hour, gangs of tough children with dirty faces, ragged clothing and bare feet, who ran and fought and dodged through the crowds like quicksilver.

"Watch yer pockets," warned Billy. "Them kids'd steal yer eyeballs if ya looked at 'em sideways."

Feeling anxious now, Christabel tugged Billy's sleeve. "Are we nearly there?"

"It's just around the corner."

Billy's aunt's shop was in a narrow two-storey terrace that looked too small to house a family. Despite its diminutive size, it seemed to be thriving, however, and a customer pushed past them as they entered. *What on earth were all these people doing shopping so late on a Friday night?* Christabel wondered.

The interior of the shop was crammed with groceries and the counter groaned under a set of scales, a huge tin of biscuits, a glass jar of rainbow-coloured boiled lollies, cigarettes for sale by the packet or individually, eggs in a basket, a wheel of yellow cheddar, and a leg of ham on a plate covered with a fly net.

Billy's aunt looked up suspiciously, then smiled when she recognised her nephew. Mary Gallagher was a small, thin, tired-looking woman with dark greying hair and sharp blue eyes. She came out from behind the counter and embraced him. "What are you doing here, William?"

"Lookin' fer Sean Rafferty, Auntie. 'E's run off with Paddy."

The bell on the shop door tinkled. A man entered furtively and gave Mrs Gallagher a meaningful look. She took a bottle in a brown paper bag from under the counter and handed it to him. He paid and scuttled out.

"Yes, I heard," she said, when the customer had left. "It's a terrible shame. It's bad enough that he's ruined his own life, without taking poor little Paddy with him." Suddenly remembering her manners, she asked, "And who's your friend?"

"Christ. . .opher," said Billy with remarkable aplomb.

"Pleased ta meetcha, Mrs Gallagher," Christabel said, lowering her voice.

The woman scrutinised her closely, eyes narrowed. *She smells a rat*, thought Christabel, and her heart thumped painfully, but the woman only said, "Isn't that Billy's cap?"

"Yes, Auntie. I lent it to 'im," said Billy.

They were interrupted by a girl in a dirty silk gown—heavily perfumed and plastered with orange face powder—who also purchased a bottle from under the counter.

"Do ya know where Sean is, Auntie?" urged Billy when they were alone again.

"Why? You're not going to do anything silly, are you?" asked his aunt, looking alarmed.

"Nah," Billy reassured her. "I promised the O'Riordans I'd ask around. Maggie Rafferty works at Altona with me."

31

Christabel was impressed with Billy's inventiveness. He had coloured, as he always did when he lied, but in the shop's dim light his aunt hadn't noticed.

"I don't know meself, but I know who will," said Mary Gallagher. "Lizzie Foy, the barmaid at the Hero. He owes her money, so she keeps an eye on his whereabouts."

They thanked her and left, sucking on gobstoppers from the glass jar.

"What were all those people buying from under the counter?" asked Christabel, as they set off down Windmill Street.

"Gawd, Miss Christabel. Did ya come down in the last shower? Auntie Mary runs a sly grog shop."

"A what?"

"She don't have a liquor licence, so she sells grog under the counter."

Christabel blushed at her own naivety. "But isn't that against the law?"

"Course it is, but she's got six kids, four of 'em still at 'ome."

"Doesn't your uncle work?"

"He can't any more," said Billy, growing exasperated. "A crate fell on him at the wharf and crushed 'is legs. If Auntie didn't work, they'd all starve."

Christabel was mortified. She couldn't begin to imagine what Mrs Gallagher's life was like with all those children and a sick husband. The only women she knew who worked were the servants who lived at Altona and, until she'd heard about Maggie Rafferty, she'd always presumed they were either unmarried or widowed. "I'm sorry, Billy . . ."

"It's all right, Miss. Ya didn't know."

They were silent for a time, then, at the risk of sounding stupid again, Christabel asked, "What's the hero?"

"A pub, the Hero of Waterloo"—he pointed—"down there on the corner of Fort Street."

When they reached the pub, Billy said, "I'll go in, you stay out 'ere. Stand against that wall and don't stare and don't talk to nobody. And don't move."

What a bossy boots! thought Christabel, but she obediently melted back into the shadows and watched as Billy elbowed his way through the heaving throng into the public bar of the Hero. At first she was nervous, afraid that someone would notice her, but it seemed that a pair of breeches, like some magic cloak in a fairy story, made people invisible. A crowd of raucous revellers circulated through the pub; the body of a Lascar with a gold earring hurtled from the door, fell in a heap on the footpath and lay still; a youth emerged, vomited in the gutter and went back in. By now Christabel was beginning to feel confident; nobody had given her a second glance. But where on earth was Billy? Had something happened to him? Just as she was about to hurl herself into the bar to find him, he emerged, his face flushed and shining. *He's been drinking beer!* thought Christabel, outraged. But she still needed Billy, so she didn't scold. "Well?" she demanded. "What did you find out?"

"Lizzie Foy reckons he's staying at the Sailors' Rest in Sussex Street with his girlfriend," Billy reported.

"Let's go and have a look," Christabel urged.

Billy was scornful. "Rafferty won't be 'ome on a Friday night."

"Maybe not, but I want to see where it is," Christabel insisted. *In case I need to come back alone.*

They made their way to Sussex Street and picked out the Sailors' Rest in a row of seedy boarding houses. Christabel sped up but, as they neared the building, Billy suddenly grabbed her arm and dragged her across the road. "Look straight ahead and walk on," he ordered.

Christabel couldn't resist a peek, of course. So that was what was worrying Billy. On the front steps of the Sailors' Rest lolled a gang of flashily dressed young men drinking from bottles in brown paper bags—perhaps from Mary Gallagher's shop. They heckled passers-by, shouting rude suggestions at women, and jostled and cuffed each other. It was the sort of situation that could easily get out of hand.

When they were safely past, Billy explained, "They're from The Rocks Push. They're Sean Rafferty's mates."

"Are they dangerous?"

"Yair, they carry razors."

Christabel shuddered. "What do we do now?"

"Even if 'e is inside, we're not gunna get past that lot. I s'pose we'll 'ave to come back in the daytime."

Christabel had to acknowledge the wisdom of this, but it was so disappointing! She'd imagined herself charging in to rescue Paddy, but instead had been defeated by a gang of weedy louts. Louts carrying razors, she reminded herself, and felt a little better.

They trudged back along Sussex Street to Market Street, circled Hyde Park, and traversed the back streets of Darlinghurst. Christabel's legs were sore and weary by the time they climbed the McElhone

Stairs to Victoria Street and cut up Challis Avenue to the McManus home.

"I'm exhausted," she moaned.

Billy snorted. "That's cos you're used to swannin' about in carriages, Miss. You'll 'ave to get a lot tougher if yer goin' to catch a thief like Rafferty."

Christabel, who'd been about to thank him, changed her mind. Insolent boy. But when he made his hands into a stirrup and gave her a boost onto the lowest branch of the fig tree, she relented, and whispered, "Thanks, Billy. I had a wonderful time."

He ducked his head and was gone.

Christabel had expected to lie awake all night relishing her adventure, sorting through all the new sights and sensations, but she was asleep the minute her head hit the pillow—though not before she'd carefully hidden her disguise at the back of the topmost shelf of her wardrobe. She was going to need it again.

chapter four

The following week, Christabel's father began leaving early for work and returning even later than usual. It wasn't till Wednesday that he put in an appearance at dinner.

It was a sultry night, and the servants had opened the French doors between the dining room and the verandah. The scent of flowers wafted indoors on a harbour breeze. Light from a Venetian chandelier shone on the mahogany table, reflecting off the crystal glasses and silver cutlery. With its pale yellow silk wallpaper, gilt mirrors and huge cedar sideboard, it was a wonderfully romantic room, and Christabel thought it a shame that her father no longer used it to entertain friends. The parties had stopped when her mother died.

Christabel thought her father looked anxious and tired. "What's wrong, Papa?" she asked worriedly. "We haven't seen you for days."

"It's nothing a girl your age need concern herself with, Christabel," Dr McManus answered curtly.

"I'm fourteen! In China I'd be married!"

The shock made her father's soup go down the wrong way, making him splutter and cough. The serving maid moved towards him to help, but he waved her away. When he'd recovered, he said, "In China you'd probably know how to make your bed and cook a meal."

Christabel was affronted. "It's not my fault I'm useless! If you would let me go to school—"

Her father glared at her. "I will not be pestered about school. You know how I feel about it. Anyway, at the moment it's probably just as well you're not gadding about . . ." His voice trailed away.

"Tell me what's happening," wheedled Christabel.

Her father sighed, then gave in. "I suppose you're old enough to know. Cholera has broken out in Surry Hills, and we're afraid it will spread to other parts of Sydney."

"What's cholera like, Papa?"

"Not at the dinner table, please," murmured Miss Swift.

But nothing would stop Roderick McManus holding forth on his favourite subject: public health.

"It's a horrible disease. It starts with a fever and nausea and develops into vomiting and terrible stomach cramps. If it's not caught in time, the patient's blood thickens and they fall into a coma."

"That's awful!" exclaimed Christabel. "What causes it?"

"Human waste leaking into the water supply."

"Yuck. Do people die from it?"

"Not always. If it's treated properly, there's a good chance of survival. But there are always deaths in an epidemic."

"Doctor, I hear that the plague has broken out on some of our shipping routes," said Harriet Swift.

Roderick McManus frowned. If the governess had heard rumours about the plague, the news must be all over Sydney by now. The last thing the Government wanted was a panic. "How did you hear that, Miss Swift?" he asked brusquely.

The governess's cheeks went pink. "From my fiancé in Suva. He says there have been suspected cases in the Pacific islands."

The doctor shrugged. "Then we can only hope it doesn't reach New South Wales."

Christabel was puzzled. The only plague she'd heard of was the locusts in Egypt in the Bible, but that couldn't be right. "What sort of plague are you talking about, Papa?"

"Bubonic plague."

"Also known as the Black Death," Miss Swift elaborated. "It broke out in Europe in the fourteenth century and again in the sixteenth. It killed millions of people."

Christabel couldn't even imagine millions of people, let alone millions dying at the same time. How did they bury them all? The conversation was starting to make Christabel feel queasy, but she wanted to keep her father talking. Sometimes it seemed as if the only time he was animated was when he was going on about repulsive diseases. "What does it do, Papa?"

The doctor resumed his lecture. "It starts with chills, fevers and headaches, then the lymph glands swell. Here . . ." He reached over to touch the side of his daughter's neck. "If it's not treated, the infection goes into the bloodstream and this causes the black patches on the skin that give the disease its name. From the bloodstream it travels to the lungs, and the victim dies."

Christabel was alarmed at the thought of such a gruesome death. "How do you catch it?" she asked.

"It's carried by the fleas on rats. That's why it travels so well by ship, because all ships have rats. When the ships dock, the rats that come down the ropes onto the wharves bring the fleas ashore. That's how the disease spreads."

"So it will come through the wharves at Darling Harbour, if it reaches here," surmised Harriet Swift.

"And from Darling Harbour, it will quickly reach The Rocks," said the doctor. "Where it will cause havoc because the houses are so crowded and dirty." The inhabitants, he explained, were crammed into squalid, decaying terrace houses or tenements. The facilities were primitive; often a row of houses shared one open lavatory that overflowed and flooded the basements with sewage, and a single tap. The back alleys were alive with rats and the houses swarmed with fleas, cockroaches and bedbugs.

From time to time the newspapers whipped the public into a frenzy about the dangers to public health posed by the constant waves of sickness that surged through the inner-city slums, but Christabel's father believed it would take a catastrophe to frighten the authorities into action. Some efforts had been made to clear some of the worst slums, but it was proceeding very slowly.

"Is anything being done to prevent the plague reaching Sydney, Doctor?" Miss Swift asked.

"I'm afraid it is difficult to get anyone in the Government, or the dock-owners, to take the threat seriously, Miss Swift," he replied heavily, "but I am doing my best."

Christabel hardly heard her father's lament. What if the plague had already reached The Rocks? Her appetite deserted her and she felt itchy all over.

"Do you have to be bitten by one of these fleas to get it, Papa?" she asked, scratching surreptitiously.

"As far as we know."

Thank heavens. She didn't think she'd actually touched anybody in The Rocks, and she hadn't noticed any fleas in her clothing . . . But Billy had pushed his way into a pub heaving with sailors! She must warn him.

"You look a bit green around the gills, Christabel," commented Miss Swift. "Are you feeling unwell?"

"I think it's all this talk about the plague. May I be excused?"

Her father nodded. "But before you go, there's something I want you do for me. On Friday, some friends of mine, Mrs and Miss Stanley, are holding a musical evening. They've asked if you'd like to attend with me. I said you would."

A musical evening with Papa's friends? How boring, Christabel thought. "Who are the Stanleys, Papa?" she wanted to know.

"As I said, they are friends of mine. They have been living in London for twenty years, but when Mr Stanley died Mrs Stanley decided to come home. They don't have many friends in Sydney yet, so I've promised to help them meet the right sort of people."

"But why must I meet them, Papa?" Christabel complained. "I'm not the right sort of people."

Out of the corner of her eye Christabel saw Miss Swift stifle a grin with her table napkin. Her father's face took on an imperious look. "Because it is my wish, Christabel. That is all you need to know."

Christabel's hackles rose. It wasn't fair! She did tedious ladylike things like taking afternoon tea with the dreadful daughters of the Honourable Maurice FitzWilliam, the Minister for Health and her father's superior. But when she tried to talk about things *she* wanted to do, like going to school, he refused to listen.

Meanwhile, her father had resumed talking. "Mr FitzWilliam introduced me to the Stanleys some weeks ago in Parliament House and asked me to help them. Mrs Stanley is his sister."

That boded ill; if they were as boring as Lavinia and Florence FitzWilliam, the evening would be quite an ordeal.

When Christabel stayed mutinously silent, her father grew exasperated. "I don't understand why you're objecting! You'll like them. Miss Stanley is charming, and she loves the theatre as much as you do. I'm sure you'll find lots to talk about."

Christabel doubted that very much—and, frankly, she didn't know why he was making such a fuss about it.

Two days later, Christabel stood impatiently in front of the big mirror in her room as Harriet Swift did up the thirty tiny pearl buttons at the back of her best dress. When she'd finished, Christabel pirouetted so that the voluminous skirt of her buttercup yellow gown belled out. Then she shook her head to make her blonde curls dance. The result of a night sleeping in rag curlers, they wouldn't last long, but with luck they'd get her through the evening.

"You are a very fortunate girl," said Harriet. "The cost of this dress alone would feed most families in Sydney for a year, and you have a wardrobe full of them."

"I know, Swiftie, but I might as well enjoy it. Anyway, they're bought with Mama's money, and she'd have wanted me to look chic. She was mad about clothes herself." She sighed. "I just wish I was as beautiful as she was."

"Give it time, Christabel. I promise you, you'll blossom."

"But it's taking so long! I still look about eleven!"

Miss Swift put her arm around her charge, and they looked at each other in the mirror. "Enjoy it while you can, Belle. I know you think it's hard being a girl, but it's much harder being a woman."

Christabel wasn't sure she believed that. She couldn't wait to grow up. When she turned eighteen and came into her fortune, she would be able do exactly as she liked. But in the meantime, it was growing late, and Billy was waiting downstairs in a spanking new buggy to take her to Darling Point. He'd drop her off, and her father, who would arrive later, would bring her home in the brougham.

Billy's eyes widened when he saw the golden gown, but he knew better than to comment. Miss Swift helped Christabel arrange her skirts in the elegant little carriage, Billy barked "Gee-up!" and Stepper minced off.

As the chestnut horse trotted up Macleay Street, Christabel quizzed Billy about Sean and Paddy Rafferty's whereabouts.

"I told Maggie's brothers 'e was at the Sailors' Rest," said Billy. "They went there, but couldn't get past Sean's mates. I reckon 'e'll have moved by now."

"So we'll have to find him all over again?" wailed Christabel.

"It won't be 'ard, Miss. Sean don't know any place but The Rocks and Surry 'ills. 'E'll be in one of 'em."

Once they'd cleared Darlinghurst Road and turned into New South Head Road, Billy couldn't resist the temptation to put Stepper and the buggy through their paces. Ecstatic to be driving the racy two-wheeler, he was determined to make the most of it.

"You're going too fast!" cried Christabel, clutching her hat, which threatened to fly away.

"I can 'andle it," Billy called back over his shoulder, but at that moment a dog ran out from Rushcutters Bay Park straight into the path of the horse. Christabel shouted a warning, but it was too late. Stepper reared up then bolted into the park, dragging the careening buggy behind him.

Seeing a tree coming at her, Christabel screamed, then everything went black for a moment. When she came around she was hurtling through the air. It seemed to take forever, but finally she hit the grass and slid forward on her back, her hands going out automatically to stop the skid. As she came to a halt, she took some deep breaths to regain her wits, struggled to her feet, and looked around.

Stepper was nearby, calmly cropping the grass, and there was Billy, lying at the foot of a huge tree. He was completely still, his right leg buckled alarmingly under him. *Oh, please God, don't let him be dead*, Christabel prayed. She hobbled over to him, knelt down and gave him a shake. It was then that she realised her hands were bleeding, but strangely they didn't hurt.

When Billy did not stir, she shook him harder. "Billy!" she cried. "Oh Billy, please wake up."

He groaned. He was alive!

"You stupid boy!" Christabel shouted, vastly relieved. "You could have killed us both!"

Her tirade was interrupted by the breathless arrival of a rotund man in a brightly checked suit.

"Leonard Tarbutt at your service, Miss," he said, his sandy walrus moustache wagging. He doffed his hat. "I witnessed the accident." Then he frowned. "You'd better leave off, Miss. He might be hurt bad."

Caught red-handed shaking an injured boy, Christabel went scarlet with embarrassment, but Leonard Tarbutt was too preoccupied with Billy's condition to notice her discomfort. "Let me take a look, Miss," he said. "I've had some experience with first aid in the African campaign." Kneeling beside Billy, the stranger prodded and poked the groaning boy. "Just as I thought. His leg's broken. We'd better get you two to hospital." He scrutinised Christabel with bulbous pale blue eyes. "Are you ambulatory, Miss?"

Christabel nodded.

Mr Tarbutt picked up Billy, who let out a shriek of pain, and placed him gently on a horse blanket in the tray of his cart, among cardboard cartons imprinted with the legend TARBUTT'S GOANNA OINTMENT.

Christabel climbed into the cart and cradled Billy's head in her lap. With Stepper tethered behind, they set off at a trot for Sydney Hospital in Macquarie Street, Billy groaning at every bump. By now the abrasions on Christabel's hands were beginning to sting, but she knew it was her own fault for taking off her gloves like a hoyden.

At the hospital Billy was admitted immediately. A nurse checked Christabel for breaks and sprains and, finding none, washed her hands and anointed them with iodine.

After the doctor and the matron learned of Christabel's identity, they agreed she could go home, where her father could observe her for any sign of concussion. Leonard Tarbutt, their Good Samaritan, had waited patiently all this time, occupying himself with writing up orders in a small notebook with a stub of pencil and, on Christabel's release, he took her back to Potts Point.

When Christabel finally tottered through the front door of Altona, she realised from Swiftie's cry of alarm, and the horrified expression on the governess's habitually calm face, that she must look a fright. While Mr Tarbutt briefly explained the accident, Christabel surveyed the damage in an ornate mirror in the entry hall. Her hat was missing and there were leaves and grass in her hair. Her gorgeous golden gown, which had miraculously cushioned her fall, was torn and grass-stained— ruined. Her hands were covered in orange patches of iodine, and her ribs had begun to ache.

Her inventory was interrupted by a muffled

exclamation from behind her. Hearing the fuss in the hall, Mrs Cadwallader had come to investigate, and Christabel was swept into the cook's suffocating embrace, before being held at arm's length. "Are you really all right, Miss Christabel?" she asked.

"Yes, Caddie," said Christabel and began to cry. It hadn't occurred to her to weep before—there was too much going on—but the distress of Swiftie and Caddie undid her. And she was mourning the demise of her golden dress.

"She'll be a bit battered and bruised, ma'am," Mr Tarbutt concluded, "but she'll be over it in a few days."

Thanking him profusely, Miss Swift said, "I'm sure Dr McManus would wish to offer you a reward for your kind services today."

But the commercial traveller refused. Instead, he bowed and handed Miss Swift a jar of his ointment. "Recommended by thousands of satisfied customers for bruises and cuts, ma'am."

Christabel remembered her manners in time to thank her saviour, and he left.

While Caddie hustled Christabel off to a hot bath with promises of a cup of strong sweet tea, Swiftie dispatched a message to Dr McManus's office in Hunter Street, as well as one to Billy's family in Erskineville.

Dr McManus must have rushed straight home on receiving the message, for Christabel was propped up in bed and still sipping at her tea, with Swiftie hovering over her anxiously, when he arrived.

"What happened, Christabel?" he asked immediately.

"A dog ran out, Papa. Stepper bolted." Christabel sniffed tearfully. "There was nothing Billy could do."

Her father's eyes searched her face. "Was he driving too fast?" he asked sternly.

Rather than tell an outright lie, Christabel sank back into her pillows and said piteously, "I don't feel well, Papa."

The ploy worked, as her father embarked on a careful medical examination.

Later that night, when she was admiring the crop of blue bruises that had blossomed on her body, it occurred to Christabel that the accident was a blessing in disguise. Of course, she was sorry that Billy had been hurt, but it was his own fault after all—and now she was free to go into The Rocks and look for Paddy by herself.

chapter five

The day after the accident, Christabel woke so stiff and sore she had to be helped out of bed, though once she was on her feet and moving about she started to feel a little better. She was rather proud of the bruises, which were now darkening, but despite her bravado, she knew she couldn't make another foray into The Rocks, especially on her own, till she'd healed.

By eleven o'clock, bored with reading the improving novel lent to her by Miss Swift, she hobbled down to the kitchen, where Mrs Cadwallader made a satisfying fuss about her injuries.

"That Billy deserves a good walloping," Caddie said, depositing a strawberry jam tart in front of the invalid.

"It was the dog's fault," said Christabel, licking pastry flecks from her lips.

The cook snorted. "Your father might believe

that twaddle, Miss Christabel, but I know boys. I've raised four."

Fortunately, before Caddie could interrogate her, Katie Cadwallader turned up.

"Miss Christabel!" she exclaimed. "You look as if you've done two rounds with a boxing kangaroo and lost."

Christabel laughed, spraying the table with pastry, then groaned. "Stop it, Katie. Laughing hurts my ribs."

"But what happened to you?"

"Billy was driving me to Darling Point in the buggy and a dog frightened Stepper and he bolted. We were tipped over in Rushcutters Bay Park."

"Is Billy all right?" Katie asked with concern.

"Broken leg," said Christabel, eyeing off the tarts cooling on the rack. "He was unlucky. He hit a tree when he got thrown out. I landed on the grass."

"The devil looks after his own," murmured Caddie.

"Where is he now?" asked Katie.

"Probably still in Sydney Hospital. They have to wait to see if he has concussion. Papa thinks they'll let him go home tomorrow."

"What about you?"

"Papa's been keeping an eye on me. But I haven't

Susan Geason

had any headaches or double vision, so he doesn't think there's anything to worry about."

"I'll drop in and see poor old Billy on my way back to town," said Katie. "I go right past the hospital."

"He's bound to be all right with that thick skull of his," remarked Caddie, removing another tray of aromatic jam tarts from the oven. "And no, you can't have any more, Miss Greedy," she rebuked Christabel. "You'll spoil your lunch."

"I'll have one," said Katie. "I'm bushed. I've spent the morning visiting old people. Honestly, they'd talk the leg off a chair."

"They're lonely," said her mother. "Most of them don't have anything but their memories. You'll be old yourself one day."

Reproved, Katie blinked and fell silent.

Christabel didn't have much to do with old people. Her father's parents were in Scotland, and she only saw her maternal grandmother—who had taken over the family sheep station near Goulburn after her husband's death ten years before—once a year. "You were going to tell me about the Salvation Army last time you were here, Katie," Christabel reminded her.

"Oh, that's right. Well, it was started by William and Catherine Booth in London about forty years

54

ago," Katie explained. "He was a Methodist, but he thought his church wasn't doing enough for the poor, so he decided to start one that did. He made it his mission to help them, not just with Jesus's message, but with food and clothes and shelter. And we don't wait for the needy to come to us; we go to them—into their houses and into the pubs and the factories and workshops."

"You go into the pubs?" interrupted Christabel. "What's that like?"

"It can be pretty scary," admitted Katie. "But people are starting to accept us. They're beginning to see that we're there to help, not to judge." She poured herself a cup of tea. "But the best thing about the Salvation Army is that it lets women do what the men do. Mrs Booth saw to that."

"I hope no daughter of mine will be preaching in public," said Mrs Cadwallader, lips pursed.

"Why not, Caddie?" asked Christabel. "Mrs Primrose is always making speeches about votes for women. Why shouldn't Katie speak in public? I think she'd be rather good at it."

Katie went pink with pleasure, but Caddie's face darkened. "It's one thing to make a speech in a hall, my girl, but quite another to be haranguing the crowd off the back of a dray outside some filthy public house in The Rocks."

Christabel's eyes widened. "Is that what you'll be doing, Katie?"

"I hope so, Miss," said Katie looking self-righteous. "I believe I've had the call to speak God's message and help his sinners."

Her mother frowned. "And anything is better than getting a real job."

That was the last straw for Katie. "If you mean drudging for a pittance in a factory, Mum, then yes, doing God's work *is* better!"

Christabel was impressed; she'd never realised Katie Cadwallader had such spunk. Clearly unwilling to fight with her daughter in front of Christabel, Mrs Cadwallader turned her back on the girls and banged pots around to vent her feelings.

Christabel, still curious, ignored Caddie's obvious displeasure. "Isn't it dangerous, Katie?"

"I suppose so. Sometimes the larrikins throw rotten fruit at us and try to chase us off."

"Have you ever seen Sean Rafferty among them?"

"I'm not sure." She pushed pastry crumbs into the shape of a cross on the tablecloth while she thought. "Yes, I'm pretty sure he was there with his mates from the Push a couple of weeks ago. They don't like us because we're temperance."

"What's temperance?"

"We take the pledge never to drink alcohol, and we try to persuade other people to sign up. It's drink that's behind a lot of the misery I see every day in the tenements."

At this point Mrs Cadwallader, who had worked off some of her vexation, conveniently disappeared into the pantry. Christabel seized the opportunity to ask Katie when and where the members of the Salvation Army held their open-air prayer meetings. If they attracted larrikins, she might find Sean Rafferty—and Paddy—at one of them.

"Friday nights, usually," the cook's daughter replied. "We were in Surry Hills last week, and this week we'll be in Cumberland Place in The Rocks. Why?"

"I'd love to come along," Christabel whispered. "I'd give anything to hear you play in the band."

Mrs Cadwallader, who could be uncannily quiet for such a large woman, returned and caught the end of the exchange. "You can forget about that, young lady. If your father heard you say such a thing, he'd lock you up till you were twenty-eight."

Watching Katie polish off a thick ham sandwich,

Christabel silently started making plans. When the young woman gathered her possessions, put her hat on and kissed her mother goodbye, Christabel rose and limped out to the gate with her.

Before they parted, Katie hesitated, then said, "You're still interested in finding Paddy Rafferty, aren't you, Miss Christabel?"

"Yes, I am," Christabel confessed. "If you see him, could you let me know?"

Katie studied Christabel's face. "What are you up to?"

"It's better you don't know, Katie."

The girl frowned. "Whatever it is, be very careful. There are some bad people out there. One of our lasses was assaulted in the Red Cockatoo in Glebe last week when she was selling copies of *War Cry*. Now we have to go into the pubs in pairs, for safety."

Having delivered her warning, Katie Cadwallader took her leave and strode off towards the Domain, sturdy and upright in her military-style uniform. When she turned to wave at top of the hill, Christabel called out, "Katie! I think you're very brave, whatever Caddie says."

There was a spring in Katie's step as she disappeared around the corner.

chapter six

On Friday night, Christabel announced that she was having an early night and retired to her bedroom at nine. The servants were in bed soon after, and she heard Harriet Swift go to her room at nine-thirty. Her father was out and would most likely return late but, now that she was recovered, he was unlikely to look in on her.

At ten o'clock Christabel donned her disguise, slipped out of the window and shinnied down the fig tree. Keeping to the shadows, she crept through the grounds and into the roadway. For the first time, she felt a small thrill of fear at what she was about to do. It was one thing to stroll around the city with Billy, but quite another to make her way to The Rocks alone.

Without Billy, the back lanes of Darlinghurst and Woolloomooloo were too daunting, so tonight Christabel kept to the busiest streets, hurrying along with her hands in her pockets and head down. As before, nobody took any notice of a teenage boy.

Worried that she'd miss the prayer meeting, she stopped to ask a kindly woman in The Rocks where she could find Cumberland Place, and discovered that she was still several blocks away. Turning a corner too fast, she almost fell over a group of noisy children dancing around in a circle, playing a game. She recognised the words—it was "Ring-a-Ring o' Roses."

> *Ring-a-ring o' roses*
> *A pocket full of posies*
> *A-tishoo! A-tishoo!*
> *All fall down!*

The ragamuffins fell in a heap, laughing. But the words seemed ominous to Christabel. If the plague did break out in The Rocks, as her father feared it would, those children might indeed fall down—but they wouldn't be laughing. A shiver ran down her spine, and her mood was more sombre as she hastened down the street.

By the time she got to Cumberland Place, the Salvation Army meeting was well under way. Stationing herself against a shop wall, her face in shadow, Christabel surveyed the scene. The crowd consisted of a group of sailors; some drunken men attracted from the pub on the far corner; a few girls in tawdry satin dresses; some shabby but respectably dressed couples who actually seemed to be listening; and dozens of dirty, squabbling children who ran in and out of the crowd squawking like parrots. They were all watching a tall, thin young man in uniform who stood on the back of a dray telling them that Jesus loved the poor man in The Rocks as much as he loved the rich man in his mansion in Bellevue Hill, and that He had come on earth to save everybody. The drunks tried to shout him down, and the sermon was punctuated by the shrieks of the street children.

The preacher soldiered on, however, and when he'd finished the band struck up. Tubas blared, the trombone moaned, and Katie Cadwallader crashed her tambourine energetically. A few voices around Christabel joined in the words of "Onward Christian Soldiers". *Perhaps this meeting would pass off peacefully*, Christabel thought, a little disappointed.

Then, out of a side street, burst a group of young men, who began shouting insults and pushing their way to the front of the crowd. The music faltered, but when the bandmaster, a middle-aged man with impressive ginger mutton-chop whiskers, raised his baton, the band struck up again, louder this time.

Christabel heard a female voice nearby say, "Sadie, ain't they from Pyrmont?"

Christabel stole a look and saw two girls about her own age, one a ferret-faced redhead, the other an attractive brunette, both dressed in flashy clothes and reeking of violet scent.

"Yeah, there's Bob Duffy, Mary's boyfriend," replied the redhead, pointing. "He loves a barney. I wouldn't want to be one o' them Bible-bashers."

She was proven right immediately. Not about to be bested by a brass band, the larrikins started hurling rotten tomatoes at the musicians. As Christabel watched in horror, one struck Katie on the chest, leaving a red stain on her uniform. Still singing, Katie looked down in dismay and tried to wipe off the mess. The band played on bravely, but the wiser members of the audience melted away, unwilling to get caught up in the violence. The larrikins regrouped and began to push forward in a wedge.

"Watch out, Reginald, they're going to overturn the dray!" shouted Katie. The preacher jumped to the ground.

Suddenly a commotion broke out at the back of the crowd, and several tough-looking men began pushing their way through the throng.

"Oh Gawd, Sadie, it's The Rocks Push," squeaked the red-headed girl. "See? That there's Bert Buckley and the 'andsome one's Sean Rafferty. Let's get out of 'ere."

Sean Rafferty! Christabel's eyes followed the pointing finger and saw a tall man with chestnut hair and a luxuriant moustache wading into his enemies from Pyrmont, an evil grin on his good-looking face and a wooden club in his fist.

The remains of the crowd began to disperse; watching the soldiers of God being pelted with tomatoes was good sport, but getting too close to a gang brawl could be downright dangerous. Christabel pressed herself back against the wall, but held her ground. Then came the ear-splitting, high-pitched sound of a whistle. A man's voice shouted, "It's the rozzers!" The brawlers paused, ears cocked, then split up and scattered. When Sean Rafferty took off, Christabel followed him.

It was difficult trailing Rafferty through the crowded streets. He was a good runner and, as Christabel was still a little stiff from her fall, she only just managed to keep him in sight. But when he'd put some distance between himself and the affray, Rafferty slowed to a walk. Heaving a sigh of relief, Christabel realised he was heading in the direction of the Sailors' Rest. So perhaps he hadn't moved yet . . .

Sure enough, when they got to Sussex Street, several of the brawlers from the Cumberland Place battle were already waiting on the front stoop of the boarding house. They called out as Sean approached, and the noise brought a woman to the window above —and a little boy. It was Paddy Rafferty!

"Come down 'ere and 'ave a drink, Jeannie," Rafferty called to the woman, and soon after she appeared at the front door with the boy. She was tall and well built, with a pleasant face, thick sandy hair and grey eyes. This must be Sean Rafferty's girlfriend.

"We need some grog, Sean," said one of the men. "Send Paddy."

"No, mate, I'm not lettin' 'im out of me sight," said Rafferty. "I don't want them O'Riordans nabbin' 'im." He looked around for an alternative and caught sight of Christabel skulking on the other side of the road, pretending to look in the window of a pawn shop. "Oi, you, get over 'ere!" he yelled.

Alarmed, Christabel looked around—he meant her!

"Yair, you! Get a move on!" Rafferty yelled.

Desperately, Christabel weighed up her options. Should she run away? But then they might chase her and discover she was a girl. She would just have to bluff it out. Besides, this was an opportunity to get close to Paddy. Heart pounding, she sidled over to the men, keeping her head down.

"Go and get us a jug of beer from the Brown Dog," ordered Rafferty, handing her a shilling. "And make it snappy."

Christabel took the money and ran to the pub on the next corner, feeling the eyes of the men boring into her back. Having never been in a pub before, she was daunted by the mass of tightly packed bodies, the stink of beer, tobacco and unwashed people, and the cacophony of singing and shouting in the Brown Dog. Taking a deep breath, she eeled her way into the crowd. The revellers were three deep at the long public bar, but Christabel managed to push her way through.

"I want a jug of beer," she said in a low voice.

"'Ow much?" asked the blowsy barmaid impatiently.

Christabel had no idea. "It's for Sean Rafferty," she said, opening her hand to display the shilling.

The woman grunted, picked up a jug and filled it with beer, handing it over with some change.

Christabel soon discovered it was harder to get out of the pub without spilling the beer than it had been to get in, but she finally forced her way through the door onto the footpath, all the time clutching the jug tightly against her body, fearing they'd kick her down the street if she spilled a drop of their precious beer.

I've done it, she thought, when she burst into the street. *I've gone into a pub, bought beer and come out alive.* Her triumph was short-lived as she heard the pounding of feet, and a swarm of rough-looking boys overtook and surrounded her. Oh no! What were they going to do? She wanted to drop the beer and run, but they had her hemmed in. She started to tremble with fear. Suddenly one of the boys grabbed the jug of beer and another wrenched the change out of her hand while the others jostled her. Then, as if summoned by a silent signal, the boys turned and began running back down the road. It had all taken only a few seconds. Sean Rafferty's mates, who'd observed this outrage in disbelief, set off in hot noisy pursuit.

Buffeted and confused, Christabel was paralysed for a few moments. But when she collected her wits and stopped shaking, she saw that the men had left Paddy in the care of Jeannie. Knowing she'd never get a better chance than this, she walked towards the stoop of the boarding house nonchalantly then, as she neared it, broke into a run. Before Sean's girlfriend knew what was happening, Christabel had grabbed Paddy's hand and was running towards the Argyle Cut and freedom.

"Paddy!" Jeannie screamed, then "Sean!" She picked up her skirts and chased after Christabel. To Christabel's dismay the woman ran like a greyhound.

Paddy, frightened, was roaring, "Dad! Help me!"

"Shut up, Paddy!" said Christabel through clenched teeth. "I'm a friend. I've come to take you back to your mother."

But the boy was beyond reason, struggling and shouting. Looking back, Christabel—who was beginning to tire—saw that Jeannie was gaining on them. Then she heard men's voices: Sean and his mates were after her now! Taking advantage of Christabel's lapse of attention, Paddy wriggled loose and ran back towards Jeannie. The woman grabbed the boy and hung on, but Sean and his friends kept up the chase and soon began to close in.

Terrified, Christabel darted into an alley and saw

salvation ahead—an open door! Hoping fervently that she was not making a serious mistake, she ducked though the door and closed it behind her. Leaning against it, she closed her eyes and waited for the pounding of her heart to subside. When she opened her eyes again, she found herself face to face with a tiny, ancient Chinese woman. Her jet-black hair was scraped into a knot on her crown and she wore a faded blue silk *cheong sam* and embroidered slippers.

Christabel looked at her despairingly. "Help me," she begged.

When the woman didn't respond, Christabel took off her cap. "I'm a girl, and there are bad men after me."

The old woman stared at Christabel, sizing her up, then nodded, crooked a finger, and led her along the hall to a heavy locked door. Taking a huge brass key from her pocket, she unlocked it. A blast of noise hit Christabel, and she saw by the light of a gas lamp that the room she had entered was crammed with small tables surrounded by Asian men and a few European men and women. Some played cards; others played a game with small tiles like dominoes. A gambling den! So this was what the newspapers were complaining about when they railed against the Chinese.

At the table in the centre of the room, a tall, thin Chinese man presided over a wheel that clattered as it turned. The man stared at Christabel with stony eyes, but the rest of the gamblers were so intent on their games that they scarcely registered her presence.

The old woman clucked her tongue to get Christabel's attention, then led her to a door at the back of the room. Unceremoniously, she thrust Christabel outside and pointed ahead. Christabel saw that the gambling den shared a backyard with another house. Before she could ask a question, the door slammed behind her and she was alone. Or was she? By the light of the moon she could see that the yard was almost filled with makeshift lean-tos constructed from bits of wood and scraps of tin. People actually *lived* in these hovels, Christabel realised with growing horror. But she couldn't worry about that now; her problem was how to make her way to the other house and through it to the next street without being caught.

The yard was full of junk, and she had to pick her way forward through piles of rubbish, old pots and pans, an iron bedstead, and bits of wood and tin. She stumbled and fell with a thump against something solid. It was an outbuilding and, judging by the terrible stench, it had an open privy. Afraid she might vomit, and no longer caring who saw her, Christabel pulled out her father's linen handkerchief and held it to her nose. Worse was to come, for the bump had disturbed hundreds of cockroaches, which spilled out of the lavatory in a noxious wave. She jumped back, shuddering. Then a great clucking arose from the inhabitants of a ramshackle chicken coop at the back of the house. Disturbed by the din, a large black rat dashed out of the coop and crossed the grass in front of her, just missing her boot. Plague! Christabel thought, muffling a shriek. She leapt backwards, dropping her hanky.

It would be a miracle if the residents of the house were not awake by now, but Christabel knew if she didn't go forward she'd be trapped. Gingerly she tried the back door of the house. It was unlocked. She opened it and found herself in a kitchen scullery. She could just make out a filthy greasy stove and a few shelves holding packets of flour, sugar, oats and salt. A big stone sink and a table with six chairs made up the rest of the furniture. On the table sat a half-eaten loaf of bread with a dish of melting butter and a plate of fatty corned beef under a fly net. The meat smelled rotten and was almost certainly maggoty.

But she was wasting time. Quaking, she crept forward into the front room of the house, and almost fell over four children sleeping on a mattress on the floor, head to toe like sardines in a tin. Looking around she saw a flight of narrow stairs leading to an upper storey. This must be the whole house, she realised: one room and a kitchen downstairs, one room upstairs, and no bathroom. For six people! She eased her way forward, trying not to clomp on the bare boards with her boots, and was almost at the front door when a noise stopped her in her tracks. It was coming from above. Glancing up, she spied a ghostly figure at the top of the stairs—it was a woman in a nightgown looking down at her. She'd been discovered!

Paralysed, the two stared at each other for a moment. The woman recovered first and shouted, "Thief! Thief!"

What thief? Christabel wondered, then went cold when she realised the woman meant her. With no need for quiet any longer, she thundered to the front door, wrenched it open and fled, clattering along the cobblestones.

Fear lent her speed and endurance, and she ran until she had a stitch in her side. Bending over, trying to catch her breath, she noticed that she was halfway home. After making sure there was nobody following her, she slowed to a walk and thought through the night's events.

She'd been so close, and then Paddy himself had sabotaged her. *Ungrateful boy*, she thought. *Here I am trying to help him, and he betrays me!* Then a quiet voice in her head reminded her that Paddy was the victim here, not Christabel. He'd had no idea who she was, and must have been petrified to find himself being abducted by a stranger. She'd also made it impossible for herself to go back to The Rocks. By now the news of the failed abduction would have gone out on the bush telegraph, along with a description of the kidnapper. If she was to save Paddy, she'd need a new plan.

As she recalled the rest of the night, she saw in her mind's eye those shanties in the backyard of the Chinese gambling den. How could anyone live in a lean-to like that—open to the rain and wind, tropical in summer and freezing in the winter? And that lavatory! She nearly gagged at the memory. And how did the people in that horrid little terrace house survive? Thinking of the comforts of her own home, where food appeared magically when it was needed and everybody had a bedroom of their own,

Christabel could not imagine sleeping four to a bed and eating maggoty corned beef. Billy had tried to warn her that The Rocks was another country, but she hadn't really understood until tonight. Living in Potts Point, on the ridge above the city, was like living in another world. She felt as if she'd been walking around all her life with her eyes shut.

But as she neared home, Christabel's mood lifted. Although she'd failed to rescue Paddy, and although she'd been frightened half out of her wits and shocked by the violence and squalor she'd seen, she was pleased with her adventure. What a pity she couldn't tell anyone about it!

chapter seven

It was the middle of the following week before Christabel had formulated a plan. But before she could carry it out, she had another engagement. On Wednesday afternoon, she joined her friend Laura at a meeting of the Womanhood Suffrage League in the public room above Quong Tart's tearoom in King Street. To her surprise, her father had approved of the outing, telling her it would do her good to learn a little about serious issues.

Harriet Swift, who was interested in women's rights, was delighted to accompany her. As it was a glorious day, they walked down through the Domain, and arrived at a quarter to four to find Laura waiting.

They took their seats and Christabel surveyed the audience. There were about sixty people present, most of whom were female and middle-aged. But there were at least three older women, a few young ladies and, Christabel counted, ten men. One young man carried a notebook and was probably a journalist. Christabel and Laura, who were the youngest by several years, gazed enviously at three women who looked like university students, though Christabel did wonder why they had to be quite so dowdy. Christabel herself had dressed carefully for the occasion in pink and white striped Swiss cotton, a straw hat with pink ribbons, white gloves, and pale green kid boots. There were only two other fashionably dressed women in this serious audience, and they looked sufficiently alike to be mother and daughter.

Mrs Primrose, who was up on the dais with several other women, waved to Christabel, then the gathering quietened and Miss Rose Scott stood to open the meeting.

Christabel had heard people say that only ugly women who couldn't attract men became suffragists, but no one would dare say that about Miss Scott. Though quite old, she was stunningly beautiful, with fine features, deep-set grey eyes and a halo of white hair.

Rose Scott spoke about the reasons why women needed the vote. "We should not have to rely on men's good will for security," she said. "If we could vote and stand for Parliament, we could elect people who would make laws that benefited women and children." Then women would be able to get a decent education and enter the professions, so they could earn their own money and be independent. That way, instead of being forced to stay in bad marriages, they could leave, knowing they were able to support themselves and their children.

To Christabel, thinking of Maggie Rafferty's case, it seemed to make a lot of sense. She looked around to gauge the reaction of the rest of the audience, and saw that they were hanging on every word. Beside her, Harriet Swift was leaning forward, listening intently. Miss Scott had also scoffed at the idea that women should not be allowed to vote because they were too stupid to understand politics. *They wouldn't think that if they heard her governess conversing with her father at the dinner table*, Christabel thought. Look how much she knew about the Black Death—not to mention history and mathematics and literature. And Christabel was quite sure that she herself was perfectly capable of understanding politics if she put her mind to it, thank you very much.

Miss Scott introduced Mrs Rowbotham, a small drab woman from the Women's Christian

Temperance League, and sat down to thunderous applause. Mrs Rowbotham became quite animated as she talked about the hunger, violence and degradation in families where the breadwinner spent most of his pay on beer. Christabel, who'd never really given much thought to these kinds of issues before, realised she'd learned something about the evils of drink in those pubs down at The Rocks. According to Mrs Rowbotham, the only answer was abstinence—no half measures. Imagining her father's reaction if he were forced to give up wine with his dinner and a brandy after it, Christabel thought the temperance women were highly optimistic.

The next speaker was Louisa Lawson, editor of the women's magazine, *The Dawn*. Pointing out that South Australia and Western Australia had already given women the right to vote in state elections, she said she was ashamed to live in such a backward state as New South Wales.

"It's a disgrace that we are still treated like second-class citizens here," Mrs Lawson said. And next year, when the colonies became the Commonwealth of Australia, she continued, women must demand the right to elect members to the new national parliament. "If the women of New Zealand can do it, so can we!"

The audience roared its approval.

Laura nudged Christabel and whispered, "She's Henry Lawson's mother. You know, the poet. Mother admires her enormously. She says Mrs Lawson's husband was a drunkard so she left him and went to work to raise her son by herself."

"She didn't do a very good job," replied Christabel. "I've heard that he drinks too."

Harriet Swift frowned and put her finger to her lips. Christabel drifted off into a daydream, only to be roused by an outbreak of applause. "Is it over already?" she asked.

"Yes," said Laura, grinning. "I'm very impressed, Belle. You managed to stay awake through the whole meeting."

"Let's pay our respects to Mrs Primrose," suggested Miss Swift.

Laura's mother seemed surprised to see Christabel at such an earnest gathering. "I didn't know you were interested in votes for women, Belle," she teased.

"I'm very interested in having my own way, Aunt Hester and, if this helps, I'm all for it," said Christabel smartly.

"Christabel, you're incorrigible," said her governess, and the older women laughed.

"Why don't you two get yourselves something to eat," suggested Mrs Primrose.

The girls made a beeline for the refreshments table, loaded up plates with sandwiches and cakes, secured a drink each, and found a quiet corner.

As she finished an egg sandwich, Laura said, "What's going on, Belle? You've been looking like the cat that swallowed the canary all afternoon."

Christabel had vowed not to tell anyone but Billy about her adventures, but the temptation to confide in Laura was simply too great. If she didn't tell someone soon, she'd burst! "You have to swear that you won't tell your mother," she warned.

Laura swore secrecy. Satisfied, Christabel told her best friend all about the disguise, the sorties into The Rocks, and about how close she'd come to saving Paddy. When she recounted her meeting with the ancient Chinese woman, Laura threw up her hands. "A Chinese gambling den!" she exclaimed.

Christabel hastily hushed her.

"Haven't you read all those stories about the Chinese in the *Herald*?" demanded Laura. "It's said they kidnap girls and sell them into slavery!"

"I know the Chinamen were gambling, Lolly, but plenty of Australians gamble, too. And the old lady

79

didn't kidnap me, she saved me. She didn't have to do that. If those louts had caught me, they would've beaten me black and blue."

"I suppose you're right," Laura conceded. "So what happened when you left the gambling house?"

When Christabel described the horrors of the backyard of the tenement house, Laura screwed up her face. "No wonder people get sick all the time. Imagine eating food out of that kitchen. Now you can see why your father's always carrying on about cleaning up the slums."

Laura listened, dumbfounded, as Christabel recounted her close shave inside the house. "Tell me you're making this up," she begged.

"It's all true, Lol," said Christabel. "Cross my heart."

"It's a miracle no one caught you," her friend said. "You're not going back into The Rocks again, are you?"

"No, I can't, not after what happened. I might be recognised. And, besides, Sean Rafferty has probably moved." Christabel didn't dare confide her fears about the Black Death.

Laura looked relieved. "Perhaps it's a sign for you to stop while you're ahead, Belle. You're not Sherlock Holmes, you're just a girl."

Christabel was about to protest—although The

Rocks was too dangerous for her now, she had no intention of giving up—but just then she saw the two well-dressed women from the audience go over to speak to Mrs Primrose. "Who are they?" she asked Laura curiously.

"Mrs and Miss Stanley. They were at our last meeting. They're new in Sydney, but apparently Miss Stanley—Lily—was involved in the suffragist movement in London."

These were the women Christabel's father had so badly wanted her to meet! Intrigued, Christabel examined them closely. Mrs Stanley, who was about fifty, was plump and pleasant looking—but Lily Stanley, wearing a skirt and blouse so simple and well-cut they had to be made in Paris, and a superb cameo brooch at her throat, was far from ordinary. She wasn't the sort of woman who'd dazzle on first sight; rather she had the kind of quiet loveliness that crept up on you—a perfect oval face, a fine English complexion, soft yellowish-brown eyes, and thick, lustrous dark hair. She looked like something out of a Pears Soap advertisement in one of Christabel's magazines. Christabel began to suspect that her father's desire to be helpful to the Stanleys was not just an act of Christian charity . . .

"How old do you think Miss Stanley is, Lol?" she asked.

"About thirty, I'd say. I wonder why she isn't married?"

"Perhaps Englishmen don't like women with advanced ideas," suggested Christabel. Until recently she would have thought the same about her father, but he'd encouraged her to attend this meeting today. Perhaps he was trying to impress Miss Stanley? That was worrying. Sometimes Christabel missed having a proper family, but she wasn't sure she liked the idea of a stepmother.

"What's wrong, Belle?" asked Laura with concern. "You've gone awfully quiet."

"I think Papa may be interested in Miss Stanley."

"Romantically interested?"

Christabel nodded. Laura put her arm around her friend. "Oh no! I couldn't imagine having a step-mother." She gave her friend a squeeze. "But your poor Papa deserves some happiness."

Of course he did. Despite their terrible battles of wills, Christabel loved her father, and now that she was older she had come to see that he was not happy. "I suppose you're right. But he's too old to be thinking of marrying again."

"He's only forty! A good age for Miss Stanley."

"You've met her, Lol. What's she like?"

Laura considered. "Quite nice, I think. No airs and graces, though they're obviously well off. You could do a lot worse."

That night Dr McManus arrived home well after the dinner hour, as he often did these days, but Christabel saw him briefly before he went out again. She was shocked at how tired he looked.

"What's happening with the plague, Papa?" she asked him. "Have there been any cases in Sydney yet?"

Her father shook his head solemnly. "No, Belle, but I suspect it's more a result of good luck than good management; it's probably just a matter of time. There has been an outbreak of scarlatina in Darlinghurst, though."

"What's scarlatina?"

"It's symptoms are a rash and a fever, and it can weaken the heart," replied her father. "It affects children mostly."

Harriet Swift looked up from the book she'd been reading. "I read in today's newspaper that they've diagnosed a case of plague in Adelaide, Doctor. Is that true?"

"Yes, Miss Swift, I'm afraid so. It may have come in on a ship from Fiji, as you feared. So it won't be long before it reaches our other ports."

"Are there any measures we can take to protect ourselves?" asked Harriet.

"Apart from keeping away from places that harbour rats, there's nothing much you can do. I wouldn't think we'd be in much danger here. It's the people who live near the wharves or in over-crowded houses with open privies and backyards full of rubbish who need to worry."

Like those houses in The Rocks, thought Christabel with dread. She had to get Paddy away from there—and soon! Luckily, she had a plan . . .

Christabel was seething with impatience as she waited for her father to leave. Before he did, he said, "Oh, by the way, Belle, the Stanleys have invited us to their house for dinner on Friday night." He was gone before Christabel could react. But she had more important things than Lily Stanley to worry about tonight. Pleading a headache, she went up to her room. Tonight was the premiere of the Gilbert and Sullivan comic opera *HMS Pinafore*, and Christabel intended to be there.

chapter eight

Disguised as a boy once more and feeling quite at home on Sydney's streets at night now, Christabel made her way to the Palladium Theatre in Haymarket. From her visit to the Palace a couple of weeks earlier, she knew that Sean Rafferty liked to prey upon theatre crowds and, since the first night of a new play always attracted an affluent audience, he should find it irresistible.

As Christabel had expected, a glittering crowd had turned out for the show, with Sydney's socialites vying to show off their finery. Many of the faces were familiar to her from the parties her mother had held at Altona before she died. *Oh no, wasn't that Mr and Mrs Primrose?* She ducked out of sight, then realised that her friend's parents were unlikely to give a ragamuffin a second look.

Stationing herself opposite the theatre, Christabel waited for Sean and Paddy Rafferty to turn up. And finally, when the crush was at its thickest, she saw them stroll in nonchalantly and begin mingling with the crowd. Afraid she'd lose sight of Paddy, Christabel moved closer, and was almost run over by a carriage in the process. The irate driver shouted at her to watch herself and git out of the way! Boys might be able to go where they pleased, she reflected, but they seemed to attract an awful lot of abuse.

By the time she'd collected her wits after her close shave, Sean Rafferty was nowhere to be seen. But wait! There was Paddy ... Stealthily she moved closer to the boy, who was loitering near a group of well-dressed theatregoers. He seemed nervous. She took that as a good sign; he hadn't turned into a hardened little pickpocket yet.

If Paddy was here, Sean Rafferty must be lurking nearby. Christabel jumped up, trying to see over people's heads to locate the boy's father; he was nowhere in sight. But she did glimpse something else that made her eyes widen in amazement—her father, chatting away with Mrs and Miss Stanley like the very best of friends! So that was where he was going ... And given that he hated musical comedy, he must be trying very hard to please Miss Stanley.

Preoccupied with these alarming thoughts,

Christabel almost missed Sean Rafferty. There he was, though, standing too close to an old woman wearing a satin gown in an unfortunate shade of puce, a ratty-looking fur stole, and what looked like the family jewels around her neck. Blissfully unaware that a pickpocket was eyeing off her handbag, the dowager was earbashing a bored, supercilious young man—her son, probably. As Christabel watched, fascinated, Sean's nimble fingers snaked into the woman's handbag and emerged with a small gold-mesh purse. Unfortunately, the son had noticed, too. He shouted a warning and tried to restrain Sean, but he was no match for a street fighter. Rafferty quickly struggled out of his grasp and began pushing his way through the crowd, cries of "Stop, thief!" ringing in his wake.

This was Christabel's chance. She scanned the scene and located Paddy again. Then, using her sharp elbows to part the crowd, she started to run. Before Paddy knew what was happening, she was upon him. He let out a startled yell, but in the general hubbub nobody noticed. Clutching Paddy by the arm, Christabel charged along the street in the opposite direction to Sean Rafferty.

Paddy screamed for help and tried to dig his heels in, but Christabel hung on like a terrier. It was like trying to drag a donkey up a hill. The rumpus attracted attention, but nobody intervened. Why would they? To the casual observer they would look like a pair of rambunctious street urchins. Finally, the struggling twosome rounded a corner and were out of danger. And there, miraculously, was a cab rank with two hansom cabs waiting in line.

The driver of the first cab turned to give them a hard stare as Christabel wrenched open the door and shoved Paddy inside. "Wylde Street, Potts Point!" she shouted, as she leapt in after the boy.

"Giddyap!" said the driver, and his woebegone old nag lurched into a fast walk.

Assuming Paddy would be too sensible to jump out of a moving carriage, Christabel let go of him. He subsided into his seat and began to bawl.

"Stop crying, Paddy," said Christabel soothingly. "It's me, Christabel McManus. I just saved you."

"Why doncha just leave me alone," wailed the boy. "I want me dad."

"Well, you can't have him," said Christabel, taken aback. "I'm going to take you back to your mother where you belong."

"Me mum don't want me, Dad reckons. That's why she leaves me with Gran."

"She has to work, Paddy," Christabel explained. "Your father spends all his money on grog and gambling, so your mum had to leave. If she didn't go out to work, you'd both starve."

Paddy mulled this over, but wasn't entirely convinced. "Did me mum send you, Miss Christabel?"

"No," Christabel admitted.

"Well then, it ain't none of yer business!"

Christabel tried to be patient. "You're not a very good thief, Paddy. If you keep picking pockets, you'll get caught. And then they'll put you in a boys' home with all sorts of horrible types."

"I don't care."

What an irritating brat! "Your mother's frantic with worry, you horrid little boy. If you don't care about her, perhaps you're better off with your father and his larrikin friends. And that Jeannie."

"Jeannie's all right," defended the boy. "She gives me lollies whenever I want them. Gran don't. She reckons they'll rot me teef."

Christabel sighed. She was beginning to regret saving Paddy. But she'd gone too far to give up now. "You'll just have to make the best of it, Paddy. You're going back to your mother. Though why she would want you is beyond me."

They lapsed into a sullen silence. Distracted by the argument, Christabel had not been watching where the cab was heading, but now she looked out the window and realised, with a shock, that the cabbie was going the wrong way. She banged urgently on the roof and shouted, "Oi, driver! You're supposed to be taking us to Potts Point!" There was no answer. Instead, the cabbie cracked his whip and the horse broke into a trot.

The drama brought Billy out of his sulk. "What's 'appenin'?" he demanded. "Where are we goin'?"

"I don't know," said Christabel. She was starting to feel a little alarmed. What if the driver was a white slaver? The newspapers were always carrying on about mysterious foreigners who abducted young girls and sold them into a life of degradation. She'd never been able to find out what actually happened to these girls, but it must be nasty or people wouldn't make such a fuss. Then she remembered that she wasn't a girl; she was a boy. Why would a cabbie want to make off with two boys? Perhaps he was a friend of Sean Rafferty's and had recognised Paddy.

"Do you know the driver, Paddy?"

Paddy shook his head.

Christabel didn't know whether to feel better or

worse. But the fact that Paddy didn't recognise the cabbie didn't mean that he wasn't one of Rafferty's criminal mates. Perhaps they were being driven straight into Sean Rafferty's clutches? When she looked out the cab window and saw the now-familiar streets and alleys of The Rocks, she became certain they'd soon be reunited with Paddy's father. Who would be very angry . . .

Her thoughts were interrupted by a shout of "Whoa, Nelly!" as the cabbie pulled into the backyard of a large three-storey house. "Ludd!" he yelled. "Get yerself out 'ere. I've got summink for ya!"

Who on earth was Ludd? Poised for flight, Christabel grabbed Paddy's hand and opened the carriage door—and fell straight into the arms of a burly man in a pinstriped suit and a bowler hat. In a trice, the man had both of them in an iron grip, one under each arm.

"Archibald Ludd at yer service," he growled, as they squirmed helplessly.

Though her heart was hammering with fear, Christabel immediately began to shout. "Get your hands off me! Help! Help!"

"No one's gunna help you 'ere, lad, so ya might as well shut yer trap," advised the giant.

He was right, of course. Christabel fell silent. The giant carried them through the back door of the house, along a corridor, and up, up, up to the top of the building, passing through a heavy mahogany door with a polished brass handle, and into a dimly lit room. The room had dark red plush curtains and a thick Axminster rug on the floor, as well as lots of ornate, highly polished furniture and a huge aspidistra on a stand. It was stiflingly hot and smelled strongly of gardenia scent. The scent emanated from a woman ensconced in a red velvet armchair, like a queen on a throne. She was quite old—older than Mrs Cadwallader, and much fatter—and her face was heavily made-up. Her false-looking yellow hair—it must be a wig, surely?—was piled high on her head, and she'd somehow squeezed into a skin-tight red satin gown. To Christabel, who'd suffered nightmares after reading *Alice in Wonderland* when she was ten, she looked remarkably like the Red Queen. She must have said this aloud, for Mr Ludd raised his fist and shouted, "Shut yer gob, you!"

Christabel shrank back in fear. This was no longer a game. Fifteen minutes earlier she'd been congratulating herself on outwitting Sean Rafferty, but everything had changed since then. Now she was hoping desperately that he'd seen them get in the cab. If not, they were sunk. She wouldn't be missed till morning, when one of the maids came into her bedroom to wake her. Vanished without a trace, she thought, imagining the headlines in the *Herald*: "Potts Point Heiress Missing."

All this time the Red Queen had been scrutinising her prisoners. "The older one is a bit scrawny but the young one looks strong," she said finally. "They'll do all right. Captain Woolley should be very pleased, Ludd. Take them to the cellar. They can help around the house while we're waiting for the *Mary Anne* to come in."

As they left the room, the woman added in a severe voice, "It's Mr Ludd's job to keep order in this house. Do exactly as he says or you will be very sorry."

Who were Captain Woolley and Mary Anne? Christabel wondered. But wait a minute—the Red Queen had said *the* Mary Anne. It must be a ship. Oh, no, they were being shanghaied! She'd heard stories about boys being abducted and put to work on ships for slave wages, and she'd read *Kidnapped*. But she wasn't a boy . . . Should she tell them? No, something warned her to hold her tongue till she knew more about these sinister people and this house.

The audience was over. Ludd marched the children down the stairs, unlocked a door, and forced them down more steps till they were in a dank, mouldy cellar. He pointed to the floor, and they sat down obediently. Then he went upstairs. Paddy was about to speak, but Christabel put her finger to her lips. Sure enough, Ludd reappeared soon after with a couple of old coats, which he threw at them, along with a dented enamel chamber-pot. When he'd been gone for about fifteen minutes and they were sure he was not coming back, Paddy said, "This is all your fault. I'm gunna tell 'em yer a girl."

"Paddy, if we stick together and keep our wits about us, we've got a chance of getting out of here in one piece," said Christabel reasonably. "But if you tell on me, you'll have no one on your side."

Paddy fell silent, then said in a small voice, "I'm scared."

"So am I," said Christabel. "I think they're going to sell us to a ship's captain."

Paddy began to cry. "I want me mum."

"I thought you didn't want to go home."

"I do now."

Softening, Christabel gave the boy a hug. "Let's try and get some sleep. From what that awful woman said, the ship hasn't docked in Sydney yet. Anything could happen between now and then."

But Paddy would not be comforted. "We'll never get out of 'ere," he sobbed.

Christabel feared he might be right.

chapter nine

It was pitch-black in the cellar, and the earthen floor was cold and damp. Paddy dropped off eventually, whimpering occasionally in his sleep, but Christabel could not settle. As she shifted uncomfortably on the hard ground, she became aware of ominous scuttling and squeaking noises. She went rigid with fear. Rats! Rats with fleas! Fleas with bubonic plague! Her skin crawled, and she pulled the smelly old coat around her like a shield, too frightened to close her eyes. *What had she got them into?* she thought miserably. Instead of rescuing Paddy, she'd led him into grave danger. These people were much worse than Sean Rafferty. No wonder the boy blamed her.

Laura had warned her to be careful, but she hadn't listened. Lolly had guessed she wasn't acting out of concern for Paddy, but out of boredom and frustration. And Maggie O'Riordan hadn't asked for her help; Christabel had just barged in. She should have left it to Paddy's uncles, she thought. They might've had to battle it out with Sean Rafferty and The Rocks Push, but at least Paddy wouldn't have been harmed. Now, because of her interference, he was locked in a dank cellar waiting to be sold into slave labour on a ship. Sailors led hard lives and died young; if that happened to Paddy, it would be all her fault.

As the night dragged on, she gave in to her worst fears. It wasn't only Paddy whose future looked grim. If she clung to her disguise, she too would end up toiling on a ship till her identity was discovered. If she admitted who she was, Ludd and the Red Queen might hold her for ransom, or sell her into slavery, or they might just dump her out in the bush. They couldn't afford to let her go for fear she'd lead the police back to them.

These dark thoughts whirled in her head till she felt dizzy. She must have fallen into a doze at some stage, however, as she was jerked into consciousness by something moving against her leg—something soft. Yelping in fright, she leapt to her feet and whatever it was ran away. Paddy moaned and stirred, but didn't wake.

After her brush with the rodent, Christabel was too upset to go back to sleep. Finally, after what seemed like a lifetime, light began to creep into the cellar through a small dirty window high above her. As the room brightened, she could see that the cellar was huge, running the width of the house. There were broken-down beds piled in one corner, tins of paint, stiff old brushes and canvas drop sheets, a tailor's dummy, a sprung sofa belching stuffing, and various other bits of broken furniture. Spotting a lumpy mattress among the debris, she vowed that if she and Paddy were still here tonight, they'd be sleeping on that, no matter how bad it smelt. And one of those wooden bedposts would make quite a handy weapon, she decided, though she suspected it would take a telegraph pole to fell Archie Ludd.

These plans were interrupted by the sound of the cellar door flying open and, from the landing at the top of the stairs, Archie Ludd bellowing, "Wake up, youse, and git yerselves up 'ere!"

The children staggered to their feet and tried to get their bearings. Christabel was stiff and her nose was stuffed up from the dust and mould in the cellar; Paddy was confused, but seemed none the worse for wear. As Ludd banged impatiently on the cellar door, they clattered hurriedly up the stairs, wondering what was in store for them.

The house was just beginning to stir. In broad daylight, Ludd was as fearsome as he'd been the night before. Without the hat, his head was as bald as an egg, and he had no eyebrows above his small, brown, pebble-like eyes. Herding them before him, he shoved them into the kitchen at the back of the house, where a slatternly woman in a dirty apron and a greasy mob-cap was frying eggs and bacon on a wood stove. A skinny girl with stringy hair, a red nose and a sniff scuttled past the kitchen door carrying a chamber-pot in each hand.

"Don't just stand there," said Ludd. "You"—he pointed at Christabel—"can come out the back and chop wood. And you"—pointing at Paddy, who was staring longingly at the sizzling frying pan—"can help Mrs Wyvill."

He grabbed Christabel by the scruff of her neck and propelled her into the backyard. Christabel looked around wildly for avenues of escape, but the yard was enclosed on all sides by fences too high to scale, and the back gate was closed and secured with a chain and padlock.

"D'ya know 'ow to chop wood?" Ludd demanded.

Christabel shook her head.

"Bloody useless," he complained, shaking his

head. Levering a dangerous-looking axe out of a stump, Ludd took a piece of firewood from a pile leaning against the shed and placed it on a block. With one mighty swing he split it in two. Then he split the halves. "Now you do it," he ordered.

On her first try, Christabel missed the target altogether, just hitting the block, but she soon got the hang of it. The axe was heavy, though, and she wondered how long she could keep it up. Finally, satisfied she was working efficiently, Archie Ludd looked at his fob watch, warned her not to stop or there would be trouble, and went back into the house. Some sixth sense warned Christabel to keep working, and sure enough, a couple of minutes later, Ludd poked his head out the door to check up on her. She knew she couldn't afford to let her guard down.

In about half an hour Christabel had produced a tidy pile of kindling, but by now the sun was starting to beat down. The axe grew heavier with every strike and blisters had begun to blossom on her palms. When she put down the axe to rest for a moment, it occurred to her that she'd been so preoccupied with trying to keep her wits about her that she hadn't given a thought to what was going on at home.

It was as if, like Alice, she'd fallen down a rabbit hole into another world.

By now her family would have realised that her bed hadn't been slept in. Her father would have had the house and grounds searched and contacted the Primroses to see if she was there. Frightened and guilty about not having stopped Christabel, Laura would tell him everything she knew, including the fact that she was impersonating a boy. Enraged, her father would gallop out to Erskineville to interrogate Billy, who would have to give him a description of what she was wearing. Her father would be tempted to thrash Billy, Christabel suspected, but she hoped he would make do with a tongue-lashing.

When all avenues had been exhausted and Christabel had not been found, Dr McManus would call in the police. As he belonged to the same men's clubs as the Commissioner of Police and the Prime Minister, the case would receive top priority. The police might even be searching The Rocks for her right now. Christabel was brought back to earth by a loud rap on a window on the top floor. She looked up and saw the Red Queen staring down at her from the throne room. The realisation that that horrible woman had been spying on her gave her goose pimples, and she took up the axe again. After about an hour, the sniffling skivvy came out with a wooden box and told her she was to come inside.

"I'm Chris," said Christabel. "What's your name?"

The girl stared at her, flushed, then stuttered, "B-b-biddy Murphy."

Christabel helped Biddy fill the box with wood, and followed her inside. In the kitchen she found Paddy devouring a bowl of porridge with a knob of butter on top. Her stomach growled: she wasn't used to working before breakfast—she wasn't used to working at all, in fact—and it had made her hungry. The cook thumped another bowl of oatmeal onto the table and told her to eat it. Christabel, who normally hated porridge, wolfed it down.

After breakfast she asked Mrs Wyvill if she could wash. The cook seemed surprised that a boy would actually want to wash, but let her use the big cement washtub in the scullery. In the scrap of broken mirror on the wall, Christabel saw a real street urchin staring back at her. Her clothes were covered in wood splinters, and her face was streaked with dirt and sweat. It wasn't till she'd washed off some of the grime with a sliver of hard yellow soap that she felt like Christabel McManus again. Checking to see that she was not being watched, she rebraided her hair tightly and pinned it back up under her cap.

When Christabel returned to the kitchen, Mrs Wyvill set her to peeling potatoes and Paddy to shelling peas. Noticing Christabel's clumsiness, the cook sighed. "'Aven't you ever seen a spud before, boy?" she asked, and demonstrated how to wash the potatoes in a bowl of water, pare the skin off with a sharp knife, and remove the eyes with the knife tip.

Christabel felt quite pleased with herself when she'd mastered this domestic art, though she doubted that she would volunteer for the chore once she got home. *If she ever did,* she thought heavily.

A tired-looking middle-aged woman trudged in and greeted the cook. She stared at the children, who stared back, then collected cleaning equipment from the scullery and set to work in the parlour. The grocer, the fishmonger and the postman visited, the fishmonger staying to gossip with Mrs Wyvill, who seemed to know him well. Archie Ludd looked into the kitchen and glared at the children, then went out, and a Chinese man with a shaved head except for a plait of hair at the back delivered a load of clean laundry. The cleaning lady brought two huge trays of dirty glasses from the parlour, and Christabel had to help her wash them in the scullery. Though they were together for at least half an hour, the woman did not utter a word. Christabel was offended at first, then remembered that she wasn't the spoiled daughter of this house, but just another servant. And she wondered how cheerful she'd be if she had to spend all day cleaning up other people's mess.

All morning Mrs Wyvill slaved harder than a navvy over the stove, and in the middle of the day Biddy staggered upstairs with a heavily laden tray for the Red Queen and Mr Ludd. As well as lamb chops with peas and the potatoes Christabel had peeled, there was apple pie and cream, and a jug of ale. The smell of the chops made the children's tongues hang out, but they had to make do with cheese and onion sandwiches and a glass of water.

There was a lull after lunch, but things livened up again late in the afternoon, when women started arriving at the house singly and in pairs, chattering like magpies. They came in all shapes and sizes. A couple of them were not much older than Christabel, some were in their twenties, and a few were even older. Who were they? Were they coming here to work? Perhaps they were seamstresses. That would explain the tailor's dummy in the cellar.

The women trooped upstairs, then came down again dressed in rather skimpy clothing. They disappeared into the downstairs parlour. While watching this parade, Christabel mopped floors, tended the fire in the stove, and fetched and carried for Mrs Wyvill. Paddy laboured away in the pantry unpacking groceries and decanting the contents into tins and bottles. Once, when Mrs Wyvill was out of hearing, Christabel whispered to him, "Grab a candle and a box of matches." He jumped slightly, but nodded. Christabel considered pocketing a knife, but decided she'd never get it past Archie Ludd.

There was a rap at the back door, and Biddy let in a skinny black man with a fedora hat and a red spotted bow tie. Shortly afterwards, the sound of lively piano music and singing burst from the parlour. This struck Christabel as odd. None of the dressmaking establishments she'd visited with Miss Swift ever had entertainment.

By dusk, Christabel and Paddy were drooping at the kitchen table, exhausted. Mrs Wyvill, who must have had one soft corner in her heart—or children of her own—took pity and gave them each a glass of lemonade and a plate of corned beef and tomatoes with huge slabs of bread. Then they had to help her prepare salad to go with the chickens she was roasting for her employer's dinner. As she sliced tomatoes and shredded lettuce, Christabel made a vow never to interfere in anybody's business ever again; it was too much hard work!

Then she saw Mrs Wyvill stiffen as she heard a rustling at the kitchen door. It was the Red Queen, swathed this time in emerald-green silk with several strands of pearls nestling on her shelf-like bosom. The room was quickly filled with the heady scent of gardenias. Christabel jumped to her feet and pulled Paddy up. She wasn't quite sure why she did this, just a feeling that she must pay close attention when this woman was nearby.

"How are they going, Ada?"

"Good as gold, ma'am," said the cook. "No cheek."

"Have they eaten?"

"Yes, marm. I think they've got hollow legs."

"In that case, it's a good thing they'll be going soon. I've heard from the captain. He'll be in Sydney in two days."

The back of Christabel's neck prickled at these words, and Paddy's sticky little hand stole into hers under the table. Ada Wyvill must have noticed their reaction, for she asked her boss if the children could go outside and play.

"I don't see why not," the Red Queen replied. Smiling malevolently, she said to Christabel, "I'll be keeping an eye on you, so don't get any ideas about climbing over the fence." She swept out in a swishing of silk skirts and petticoats and a blast of scent. Christabel thought she'd never be able to smell a gardenia again without feeling ill.

When the cook gave the signal, Christabel and Paddy stampeded along the corridor and into the back-yard. It was still light outside, and the fresh air was miraculous after the heat and frying-fat smell of the kitchen. Christabel had no intention of playing, however. She drew Paddy into the shadow cast by the shed and said, "Quick! Give me the candle."

When Billy pulled it out of his pocket, she fetched the axe and cut off a small piece, hiding the rest in the woodpile. She took three matches from the box, tore off the sulphur strip, and hid the remains. Then she put both the candle stub and the matches in her boot, under the arch of her foot. That reminded her of the pound in her other boot—which gave her an idea . . .

Paddy was watching all this with admiration. "You'd make a good dipper," he observed, and Christabel was oddly pleased.

They threw themselves down on the grass, groaning with relief. But their joy at escaping from the kitchen didn't last long.

"I don't like it 'ere," said the boy.

"I'm not exactly ecstatic about it myself, Paddy. I've never worked so hard in my life." She examined her hands. They were covered in small knife nicks, and a couple of blisters had burst. If she stayed here much longer, she'd end up looking like Biddy.

"I 'ope Dad's lookin' fer me," said the boy. "Or me uncles."

"The O'Riordans?"

"Yair. They found us at Jeannie's place, and tried to get in, but Dad and 'is mates bashed 'em with beer bottles."

"Why didn't you run away?"

The boy shrugged. "I'm a bit scared of Dad. 'E shouts a lot."

"So you'd be happy to go home to your mother and grandmother?" asked Christabel.

Paddy nodded. "What are we gunna do?"

"Our best chance is to make a run for the front

door when Mrs Wyvill's busy with one of the tradesmen tomorrow. The fishmonger, I think. They seem to be old friends. They'll be too busy gossiping to watch us."

"What if Ludd chases us?" asked Paddy.

"We'll worry about that if it happens," said Christabel. But Paddy was right—the prospect of being pursued by Mr Ludd was the stuff of nightmares.

It wasn't Mr Ludd who came to get them when it began to get dark, but Biddy. Her cheek bore a red hand-shaped mark, and she'd been crying. "Mr Ludd wants ya," she muttered.

Christabel felt a rush of pity for the girl. She couldn't help having rabbity eyes and a drippy nose. And if she were being mistreated, she might agree to help them. "Who hit you, Biddy?"

"Mr Ludd," she answered. "Mrs Noad told 'im I was too slow answerin' 'er bell." So that was the Red Queen's name: Mrs Noad. Christabel stored it away to give to the police—if they ever came.

"When do you get off work, Biddy?"

"About midnight. I 'ave to 'elp get supper fer the girls."

"Do you ever leave the house?"

"I get Sunday afternoon off."

That was too late: they'd be in the captain's clutches by then.

"Don't you ever sneak out?"

Biddy paled. "Never. Mrs Wyvill would tell Mr Ludd, and 'e'd beat me. And dock me pay. I couldn't do it to Mum. The other kids'd go hungry without me wage." She was becoming agitated. "You'd better get a move on," she said. "Mr Ludd don't like to be kept waitin'."

When they went inside, Christabel could hear music, singing and deep-voiced laughter coming from the parlour. There seemed to be a party going on, with men in attendance. As they neared the cellar door, the front doorbell rang and, after telling them to stay put, Mr Ludd left them to let two men in. They were well dressed, and looked like prosperous businessmen, Christabel observed. The Red Queen certainly had a wide circle of friends.

After patting them down to make sure they hadn't stolen anything or pocketed a weapon, Archie Ludd shoved the children down the stairs. As Christabel had hoped, he didn't look in her boots. She didn't blame him; a street urchin's boots would daunt the stoutest heart. Then the cellar door banged shut and they were locked in again.

When she was sure Ludd had gone, Christabel retrieved the candle stub and lit it, and with Paddy's help dragged a mattress out from the pile and onto a clear patch of floor. They lay down, and Paddy began to snore almost immediately. Christabel was tired herself, but she had too much to think about to sleep just yet. Her mind turned to home. She and Paddy been gone a night and a day now, and their families would be frantic. And it was all her fault. She'd been determined to do what she wanted without a thought for anyone else's feelings—or their welfare. Paddy was a prisoner; Laura would be in trouble with her parents for not revealing what Christabel was up to; and Billy would be under a cloud for helping her. He might even lose his job.

And poor Papa; first her mother, and now this—he'd be so upset. *I have to get out of this alive for Papa's sake,* Christabel thought. *And when I do, he'll kill me himself.* She gave a small snort of laughter that was perilously close to a sob. Then she shook herself; if she gave into self-pity, she and Paddy were finished. She snuffed out the candle, and was almost instantly asleep.

chapter ten

When Christabel awoke next morning, every bone in her body ached, and her hands stung where the blisters had burst. She longed for a hot bath, but such luxuries were a million miles away in Potts Point. Paddy was reluctant to leave his bed, too; despite his complaints about his grandmother, she evidently didn't work him as hard as Mrs Noad and Mr Ludd did. But when Ludd roared at them from the top of the stairs they scrambled out of their fusty bed, pulled on their boots and scurried up the stairs.

Christabel thought Mr Ludd looked a little peaked this morning. Though he cuffed Paddy when the boy dawdled, he was quieter than usual, and looked a little bleary-eyed. After depositing his prisoners in the kitchen, Ludd left the house. Breakfast was porridge again, and again Christabel ate every oat. With the doorman gone, she was spared more wood chopping, which was a blessing, as the very thought of wielding an axe with her raw and tender hands made her wince. It was torture enough immersing them in cold water to peel potatoes.

When the tradesmen made their calls, she watched like a hawk. With Ludd out of the way, her plan began to look feasible. It all depended on Mrs Wyvill being distracted by the fishmonger, who was due at about eleven. But to Christabel's chagrin, at half-past ten according to the clock on the kitchen wall, the cook ordered her into the parlour to help Mrs Grimshaw, the cleaning woman. Christabel wanted to scream with frustration.

The parlour was impressive, if a little overdone. It was a spacious room with high ceilings, a grand fireplace, a sparkling crystal chandelier, and tall bay windows with deep green velvet drapes trimmed with gold tassels. A good German piano took pride of place among small ornate tables and gilded chairs.

Mrs Grimshaw swept and polished the wood floor, ran the carpet sweeper over the rugs and dusted furniture. Meanwhile, Christabel collected empty glasses and beer bottles. It was like a treasure hunt, for they lurked in every nook and cranny—on tables, on the floor, on the windowsill, under the sofa and even on the piano. The room stank of stale beer and old cigar and cigarette smoke.

Christabel put as many glasses and empty bottles as she could carry on a tray and made her way carefully towards the scullery. Only when she tripped on the hall runner did she realise how foolish she'd been to overload the tray. She frantically tried to regain her balance, but several of the glasses toppled and fell to the floor with a crash that propelled Mrs Wyvill out of the kitchen like a shot from a cannon.

"You stupid boy!" she scolded. Turning towards the staircase, she shouted, "Biddeee! Come 'ere at once!"

Biddy scuttled down the stairs, noted the wreckage, and eyed Mrs Wyvill fearfully.

"'Elp this clumsy oaf clean up that mess," the cook ordered, and marched back into her domain.

As they crouched on the floor and began picking up shards of glass, heads close, Christabel saw her opening. "Biddy, do you want to earn a pound?" she whispered.

Shock made the girl sit back on her haunches. "A pound!"

"Keep your voice down," hissed Christabel. "Well, do you?"

"What do I 'ave ta do?" Biddy asked finally.

Christabel let out her breath. "I want you to sneak out and go to the police station."

Biddy's jaw dropped. The police were the natural enemies of the denizens of The Rocks. It was like asking a gazelle to enter a lion's den. Christabel rushed on before Biddy's fear paralysed her. "You have to tell them where I am."

The maid looked sceptical; why would the police care about this nondescript boy?

Christabel looked at the other girl, assessing her. Could she be trusted? She'd have to take the risk. "I'm not a boy at all," said Christabel. "I'm a girl." She took a look around to make sure no one was lurking nearby, then pulled off her cap to display her yellow braids.

Biddy's eyes widened. "'Oo *are* you?"

"My name is Christabel McManus, and I've been kidnapped," Christabel explained urgently. "They're going to sell me and Paddy to a ship's captain tomorrow."

"But what . . . why are ya dressed like a boy?"

"I don't have time to explain," Christabel said impatiently. "Will you do it?"

"I can't," said Biddy, close to tears. "Mr Ludd would kill me."

"But he's not here. I saw him go out."

Christabel watched the girl thinking it over. Why wouldn't she do it? Perhaps a pound wasn't enough. "Biddy, my father is rich. If you save me, he'll give you a huge reward."

Still Biddy didn't seem convinced. Why on earth not? Then it dawned on Christabel: the girl could not imagine a big reward. What would persuade her? Christabel had a flash of inspiration. "And he'll give you a job in our house. We've got lots of servants, and nobody ever gets a beating."

The girl gazed into Christabel's eyes, trying to decide if she was telling the truth. Feeling her weakening, Christabel pulled off her boot, took out the pound note, and pressed it into her hand. "Please, Biddy."

Biddy stared at the pound as if it were a bomb about to explode, then closed her hand over it. "I'll try," she said.

"Sneak out when Mrs Wyvill is talking to one of the tradesman," advised Christabel, then fell silent and began picking up glass as she heard footsteps approaching.

"Why are youse two takin' so long?" the cook demanded. "We 'aven't got all day!"

Christabel was on tenterhooks for the next hour, afraid that Mr Ludd would return before Biddy could get away. But when the fishmonger arrived, and Mrs Wyvill dropped her guard, Christabel— watching from the parlour window—saw Biddy slip through the front door. She prayed Mrs Wyvill would not miss the girl and raise the alarm.

Mr Ludd arrived home at about five in a terrible temper, and thundered up the stairs to see the Red Queen. Shortly after, the sound of raised voices reached the kitchen. What was happening? Had he seen Biddy on the street? Her ruminations were rudely interrupted when Mr Ludd pounded down- stairs and into the kitchen. Seizing Christabel and Paddy by the arms he dragged them to the cellar door and shoved them roughly down the stairs, caution- ing them not to make a peep. Then he slammed the door and they heard the sound of the key in the lock.

"What's 'appenin'?" asked Paddy, wide-eyed.

"I don't know," said Christabel, "but they're worried. Maybe Mr Ludd saw your father or your uncles hanging around outside and got the wind up."

The boy's face brightened momentarily, then fell. "I want me mum," he wailed, and began to bawl.

117

Christabel's first instinct was to shake him to stop the dreadful noise, but she didn't have the heart —he had been so brave for such a small boy. And to be honest, she was beginning to feel like a good howl herself. *How much longer could she stand the constant fear and suspense?* she wondered. *And what was happening at home?* To think that tonight she and her father were supposed to visit the Stanleys at Darling Point. That life seemed a million miles away.

Christabel and Paddy languished in the cellar for what seemed like hours, Christabel in a high state of anxiety; Paddy in silent misery. Eventually, Paddy fell into a doze. Suddenly there was a great banging and crashing above. What could it be? The police? The O'Riordans? Sean Rafferty and his mates?

Christabel scrambled up, grabbed the bedpost she'd hidden under her mattress and stared up at the cellar door. Abruptly, the hubbub died down. Christabel waited, scarcely breathing. She could hear her heart thumping. Then the cellar door flew open with a crash, and there was Archie Ludd, silhouetted against the light. Paddy took refuge behind Christabel, clinging to her coat. She tightened her grip on her weapon and tensed, poised to fight, poised to run.

Ludd lumbered down the stairs towards them, looking impossibly huge, blocking the light from the doorway. On the second last step, he stopped. To Christabel's surprise, he swayed and came crashing the rest of the way down. Clutching Paddy to her, she leapt out of the way as Ludd hit the floor with an almighty thud. As the giant lay motionless on the ground, Christabel eyed him uncertainly. Was this real, or was Ludd playing some horrible game? Would he grab her ankle if she made a run for it?

"Is 'e dead?" asked Paddy in wonder.

Christabel didn't know, but she knew they had no time to lose. "Come on, Paddy! Let's get out of here."

She grabbed the boy's hand and they flew up the stairs and into the corridor. As they ran for the front door, Mrs Wyvill came out of the kitchen, wiping her hands on her apron. "What are you—?" she began.

"Ludd's fallen down the stairs," shouted Christabel, as she barged past the cook with Paddy close behind. Mrs Wyvill gave a little scream and ran to the cellar door.

Fear made Christabel's fingers clumsy, and she fumbled with the key in the lock, but finally it turned, and she wrenched open the front door. They were free!

119

Christabel looked around, but didn't recognise the street or any landmarks. Which way should they go? Then an ear-splitting human whistle rent the air. It must have been a signal, for men came running from every direction.

Paddy recognised them first. "It's Dad!" he yelled. Christabel thought the boy might run after his father, and tightened her grip on his hand. But the last two days must have changed him, for he didn't bolt. Ignoring the shouts from behind to stop and the pounding of feet, he followed Christabel as she took off along the street.

Arriving at an intersection, Christabel hesitated, afraid to take a wrong turn and end up deeper in The Rocks. And then—was she dreaming? No, it was the sound of brass instruments and the boom of a drum. There, as if by the grace of God, was the Salvation Army band emerging from a side street and marching towards her. In the front row was Katie Cadwallader, crashing her tambourine.

"Katie!" shouted Christabel. Katie looked around in confusion. Who was this boy shouting her name?

Of course! Katie wouldn't recognise her. Christabel took off her cap, revealing her braids. The look of incomprehension on Katie's face turned to one of astonishment, then determination. She said something to the men beside her, and the band quickened its pace. Dragging Paddy behind her, Christabel ran towards them. The navy blue army parted like the Red Sea to surround the two fugitives, and marched on.

The warriors of The Rocks Push rushed at the flanks of the band like dingoes worrying a flock of sheep, desperate to get their hands on Paddy. Just then another whistle, a mechanical one this time, rent the air. "It's the constabulary!" shouted the bandleader.

Sean Rafferty's mates recognised the sound too, for they immediately abandoned Paddy and fled.

Then a deep voice shouted, "Git Rafferty!"

"That's me Uncle Bernie!" Paddy cried.

So the O'Riordans were here too. But what was going on? Too small to see from the centre of the crush, and determined not to be cheated out of this spectacle, Christabel elbowed her way to the edge of the band to watch, still holding fast to Paddy.

A mad procession rushed by: The Rocks Push, headed by Sean Rafferty, were in the lead, followed by another group of rough-looking men, evidently the O'Riordans. The police were in the rear.

Christabel felt a wave of relief wash over her. She was safe at last.

The band marched on till it reached the George Street police station, where it delivered its catch to the authorities. To the stirring refrain of a martial hymn, Christabel marched into the police station holding Katie by one hand and Paddy by the other. "I am Christabel McManus," she announced to the constable on duty, "and this is Paddy Rafferty."

chapter eleven

As Christabel's abduction was the talk of the town, a senior police officer arrived at a trot and took charge. On his direction, the children were put in an interview room, with Katie Cadwallader along to dispense moral support and cups of hot sweet tea, and a message was dispatched to Dr McManus. While they were waiting, two policemen came in. The older officer, a tall, burly man with lots of gold braid on his uniform, introduced himself as Superintendent Hunter and the younger policeman as Constable O'Reilly. They sat down, the constable opened his notebook, and the superintendent asked Christabel where she had been for the last two days.

Christabel started the story; Paddy jumped in whenever she drew breath; and Katie finished it.

The superintendent shook his head in disbelief. "I hope you two realise how lucky you were," he said. "But you, Miss"—he pointed an accusing finger at Christabel—"had no business kidnapping small boys." He turned to Paddy. "And you, boy, should have taken yourself to a police station and gone home to your mother, instead of consorting with thieves." As he got up to leave, he fired one last shot at Christabel and Paddy, who by now were cowering in their seats. "If either of you shows your face in my police station again, I'll lock you up. And thanks to Biddy Murphy, there is a team of police on the way to Mrs Noad's house right now."

Christabel, who had expected some sympathy, and perhaps praise for their daring escape from the kidnappers' den, was mortified—and worried. "What will Papa say, Katie?" she whispered. "Will he be angry too?"

"Of course not, Miss Christabel," Katie assured her. "He'll just be pleased to have you back, safe and sound."

Ten minutes later there was a commotion, and Christabel heard her father's voice outside. Then Dr McManus exploded into the room and swept her into a hug. "Thank God, you're safe!"

She felt faint with relief—she wasn't going to be punished. But when the doctor held her at arm's length, and she saw traces of tears on his cheeks, her relief turned to shame. Then the dam broke, and all the fear and uncertainty of the last two days gushed forth. Christabel began to sob uncontrollably. Her father enveloped her in a hug. "Oh Belle," he said. "Where have you been?"

Then the whole story spilled out. How Christabel had gone to the theatre vowing to get Paddy back; how they'd been kidnapped by the cabbie and imprisoned in a cellar in The Rocks; and how they'd escaped. When Christabel described Mr Ludd's collapse, her father looked alarmed. Excusing himself, he hurried off to confer with the superintendent.

In the carriage on the way home, Christabel's father told her that bubonic plague had broken out in The Rocks while they were imprisoned in Mrs Noad's house. Arthur Paine, a carter, had been diagnosed with the plague and sent to the Quarantine Station at North Head. When Christabel and Paddy reached Altona, he said, the whole household would have to be quarantined under his care until the children could be declared clear of the disease. Remembering the rats in the cellar, Christabel went cold all over, but she decided not to tell her father; he was worried enough already.

Arriving home, they found the whole household —including Maggie Rafferty—waiting for them. Harriet Swift ran to embrace her charge, and they both shed a tear, then Caddie enveloped Christabel in a hug that left her covered in flour.

Maggie and her son had a rapturous reunion. "I can't thank you enough, Miss Christabel," said Maggie when she heard what had happened.

Then, at Dr McManus's insistence, Christabel and Paddy were each plunged into a very hot bath and scrubbed, and their clothing was burned.

Christabel did not see much of her father for the next couple of weeks. But she couldn't resent his absence this time, for he was organising the campaign to contain the threatening epidemic. The Rocks, Millers Point and the Darling Harbour wharves were barricaded off and the whole area was placed under quarantine while plans were made for a massive clean-up of the affected areas.

When he finally found a spare hour, Dr McManus and Christabel met in his study to discuss her future.

"I've decided to let you go to school with Laura

in the new term, Belle," he began, though he had to stop when Christabel rushed over and flung her arms around him. Extricating himself, he continued, "I've spoken to Miss Swift about it, and she agrees with me that it would be the best thing for you."

"But what will Swiftie do, Papa?" Christabel asked, suddenly concerned. She had never stopped to think that her beloved governess might be inconvenienced by her plans. "Where will she go?"

"She's decided to join her fiancé in Suva. I suspect she was just waiting for the right opportunity."

Christabel's relief was premature, though, for her father was not quite finished. "In exchange, I want some promises from you," he said.

Christabel guessed what was coming. In the long, dark hours in the Red Queen's cellar, she'd spent a lot of time brooding about her own selfishness and impetuosity, and the consequences for those she loved. "Yes, Papa," she said meekly.

"You have to promise me you will try to behave like a lady. That means no more dangerous adventures."

"Yes, Papa."

"And I want you to meet Miss Stanley, and show her every courtesy, because I care for her."

127

This was unsettling news, but Christabel knew better than to argue. "Yes, Papa." If she didn't get on with Lily Stanley, she thought, she could always leave when she turned eighteen and go to Paris.

Her father cleared his throat and looked uncomfortable. He rose and rearranged some books on the bookshelf, then sat down and fiddled with his fob watch. Christabel was bemused. What on earth was wrong with him?

At last he said, "I know that I've neglected you, Belle. I was so distraught when your mother died, it seemed easier to bury the grief than to face it. I found I could do that by focusing all my energy and attention on my work. But I see now that I didn't take your feelings, and your grief, into account. So I'm going to make you a promise. From now on, I'll be a better father and spend more time with you."

Christabel was flabbergasted. She had felt so lonely since her mother had died—and her father's withdrawal, both physical and emotional, had only increased her loneliness. She didn't know whether to laugh or cry, so she just threw herself into his arms and said, "Oh Papa, I've missed you."

They talked for a while about Christabel's plans for school and her father's plans for cleaning up The

Rocks and, when the right moment came, Christabel put some requests to him. She wanted a job for Biddy Murphy, lenience for Billy Brownlow, and a place for Paddy Rafferty at Altona. In his new mellow mood, her father agreed to them all.

When he left, and Christabel could think clearly again, it occurred to her that, even if she had done the wrong thing, it had certainly turned out right. As Caddie always said, There's more than one way to skin a cat, Miss Christabel.

postscript

By the time Christabel and Paddy were on their way home from the George Street police station, a squad of policemen had raided the Red Queen's house. Too heavy for the women to move, Archie Ludd was still lying on the floor of the cellar when they arrived. The police surgeon diagnosed bubonic plague, and Ludd was taken to the Quarantine Station for treatment. He recovered, but when he was arrested and charged with kidnapping, thanks to Christabel's statement to the police, he may have wished he hadn't.

The Red Queen, Mrs Irma Noad, was also charged with kidnapping. Captain Woolley, for whom she'd taken the children, was investigated and charged. Sean Rafferty disappeared, and was later sighted in New Zealand.

From the reports of Archie Ludd's trial in the *Herald*, Christabel learned what had happened after she'd taken Paddy from the theatre. Sean Rafferty had chased after her and seen them get into a cab. Eventually, he had tracked down the cabbie and beaten the truth out of him. The commotion she and Paddy had heard upstairs just before they escaped was Sean Rafferty and his gang trying to break in. Mr Ludd had repelled Rafferty's attack on the front door, but Mrs Noad ordered him take the children into a neighbouring house through the attic and hide them elsewhere. Fortunately for Christabel and Paddy, this plan was foiled by Ludd's collapse. The O'Riordans, who'd been shadowing Rafferty, had been planning their own attack on the house when the children escaped.

After the story of the kidnapping and rescue appeared in the newspapers, Katie Cadwallader became a celebrity. Now when she went into hotels selling copies of *War Cry*, she was treated as a heroine and swamped with donations instead of ridicule. She took up public speaking and proved to be very good at it, as Christabel had predicted. Eventually her mother relented and went to hear her preach in the Domain. Caddie was spellbound by Katie's dramatic account of how God, in the form of the Salvation Army band, had intervened to save Christabel McManus and Paddy Rafferty from a gang of violent larrikins after they had escaped from their confinement in a house of ill repute.

After a few months under Mrs Cadwallader's wing at Altona, Biddy Murphy lost her sniff, put on weight, blossomed and developed a crush on Billy Brownlow, who had been reinstated as stable boy as part of Christabel's agreement with her father.

Arthur Paine, the first victim of bubonic plague in Sydney, died at the Quarantine Station. The outbreak of plague in 1900 was not confined to The Rocks, though the area got most of the blame; cases were also diagnosed in Redfern, Surry Hills, Glebe, Woollahra and elsewhere. Although hundreds became ill, only 103 people died of the disease. Nonetheless, the populace was frightened by the plague's terrible history. The newspapers ran emotive headlines about "The Black Death", and the public began clamouring to be vaccinated. On one March day alone, two doctors inoculated one thousand people. In their hysteria over the plague, people overlooked the grim fact that common diseases such as diphtheria, whooping cough, tuberculosis, typhoid and dysentery took a much greater toll. Between 1875 and 1900, dysentery killed 8552 people in Sydney.

The epidemic forced the City Council to intensify the program of slum clearance that had started thirty years earlier. Houses, streets and even whole neighbourhoods in inner Sydney were demolished and rebuilt. Meanwhile, between March and July 1900, nearly four thousand premises in the plague suburbs were cleansed, disinfected, lime-washed and fumigated. War was declared on rats, and nearly thirty thousand were trapped, and their carcasses destroyed at the quarantine depot in The Rocks.

Some believed the demolition of inner-city neighbourhoods was not necessary, and that the outbreak of plague was caused not by unhygienic housing but by the noxious state of the wharves in Sydney Harbour. And indeed, when the wharves were cleaned up, over fifty thousand tonnes of silt and sewage was dredged and removed, and close to thirty thousand tonnes of garbage was dumped at sea, with another twenty-five thousand tonnes burned. Nearly fifteen hundred dead animals were removed from the harbour, the disgusting haul including the putrid carcasses of rats, cats, fish, fowls, parrots, sheep, pigs, calves, hares, kangaroos, rabbits, flying foxes, sharks and even a bullock.

Paddy Rafferty stayed on at Altona with his mother, sharing the stables attic with Tom Cartwright and Billy Brownlow. After the ordeal they had lived through together, he became completely devoted to Christabel.

In 1902, women in New South Wales won the right to vote in state elections, and Australian women gained the right to vote in federal elections.